FULL IRISH MURDER

A FIONA MCCABE MYSTERY

KATHY CRANSTON

Fiona McCabe had just taken her finger off the buzzer that connected to her brother's shop when the phone rang.

"McCabe's," she said, almost certain it was Marty calling to tell her to stop distracting him.

"Fi, it's Ben."

She frowned. "What's up? Are you ringing about the buzzer? It's grand. I thought Marty was working there—I was only buzzing him to come over for a cuppa."

Ben had recently—and reluctantly—started working at Marty's hardware shop next door. Fiona wished she hadn't mentioned tea: Ben would close up the shop and sit in the pub for the whole afternoon if she gave him the chance.

She was about to hang up when he muttered her name again.

"It's okay, Ben. There's no emergency. To be honest, I only use it to invite Marty over for tea. Thanks for checking. How's everything going in the shop?"

"How should I know?"

She sighed. Ben hadn't inherited the same work ethic as the rest of them and sometimes it grated on her. "There's no need to sound so enthusiastic. You should be grateful to have the job."

"I am," he snapped. "Of course I am. But I have no idea how the shop is. I'm not rostered to work again until Thursday. Anyway, Fi—"

She shook her head, amused by the timing. "That's funny, Ben. I just buzzed Marty for tea and you rang a second later. I honestly thought—"

"Fi!"

She finally noticed the panic in his voice. Fiona's jaw clenched. She'd never heard Ben sound so stressed before. "What is it, Ben? What's happened?"

"It's Mam," he hissed. "She's been arrested. You've got to come over. I don't know what to do."

"What?" The idea of her mother being arrested was ridiculous. "You seriously think you can fool me that easily?"

"Ben?" she added when he didn't respond.

"Fiona, come home. They're just after taking her."

"*Who's* after taking her?"

Ben sniffed. "All of them. Fitzpatrick, Conway and Sergeant Brennan."

"But why?" Fiona asked. "The woman obeys laws that don't even exist in Ireland. What could she possibly have done?"

Then she heard the dial tone. He'd hung up. She realised with a sinking feeling that this was no joke.

"Oh good God," she cried, reaching for her keys and phone. "What's after happening now?"

The door opened just as she was running out from behind the bar.

"Where are you off to?" Marty asked as he sauntered into the pub. "I thought you buzzed me for a cuppa. It's awful quiet in the shop—I wish they'd put on a new DIY show on the telly. That always gets the crowds in—"

"Come on," Fiona interrupted, grabbing his arm and hurrying towards the door. "We've got to go!"

TEN MINUTES LATER, they were bursting through the door of their parents' house. It was strangely quiet: the place was usually hectic morning, noon and night thanks to the fact that six out of the seven McCabe children lived there or close by and were always calling over.

"Hello?" Fiona called, feeling an awful sense of foreboding.

Ben appeared in the doorway of the sitting room just as she was about to leave and go look for them at the Garda station. "There you are. It's about time."

"What are you talking about? I came as soon as I hung up the phone!"

"Don't mind him, love," said a weary voice behind them. "He's probably in shock. I know I am."

Fiona spun around. "Dad! What are you doing here?"

Francis McCabe sighed. "Someone has to sort this mess out. I'm trying to get in touch with the solicitor and she's told me she wants the human rights commission informed and God alone knows who else." His shoulders slumped as if he didn't have the faintest notion what he ought to be doing.

Fiona stared at him. She'd never seen him like this. Francis McCabe was usually the kind of man who leapt into action at the slightest hint of trouble. He'd presided over the PTA of Ballycashel National School for over a decade while his children were taught there. He was unflappable—or so she'd come to believe.

"Oh my God, Dad," she gasped, unable to believe

what she was seeing. "Please tell me you've got this, that you know what to do."

He glared at her. "Of course I don't know what to do. Margaret's done a lot of odd things in her time, but getting arrested for murder?"

Fiona's jaw dropped and she groped behind her for something to steady herself against. "Murder?" she repeated, the word feeling strange in her mouth, especially when she was using it in relation to her God-fearing, law-abiding mother.

She had assumed it was all a mistake; that her mother had been arrested for some minor infraction. After all, Sergeant Brennan, the most senior police officer in Ballycashel and Fiona's arch-nemesis, had built quite a reputation for being trigger-happy when it came to prosecuting minor crimes. Fair enough, Margaret McCabe had threatened assault on a few occasions, like when she had narrowly lost out on the bingo jackpot one Saturday night and then returned to find her children had demolished the roast beef they were due to have for Sunday dinner.

But murder?

Murder?

"Dad?" Fiona said, stumbling into the sitting room and collapsing onto the couch. "What's going on? Mam wouldn't hurt a fly."

He followed her in and sat down beside her. "I

know, love. I know. I should be out there shouting from the rooftops and getting her out. The truth is I'm stumped. I've never had to deal with a situation like this."

"But Dad," she whispered, squeezing his arm. "There's been a lot of stuff you've had to figure out. Like that time Colm stuck a pitchfork through Ben's foot. And sure didn't you become a dab hand at sticking us all back together with plasters instead of making yet another trip to the A&E?"

He shook his head morosely and let out a terrible sigh. "That was different."

"How? You're not a doctor. It's no small thing to put your children back together again."

"Like humpty dumpty," Ben said, leaning against the doorframe and beaming as if he'd come out with something insightful.

"Not helpful, Ben. Dad, come on. We'll fight this."

But Francis McCabe wouldn't be encouraged. He sat there slumped, staring at the blank TV screen. "That was different. I had Margaret to help. We figured it out together. Now…" He shook his head. "I know I'm letting her down, but I just can't work out what to do. She doesn't want me down there; she's too embarrassed."

"Ah, Dad," Marty said. "I'm sure she's not."

"She is."

"Right," Fi said, jumping to her feet. "This is crazy."

"Where are you going?" her father and youngest brother asked in unison. Marty said nothing: he had already turned towards the door.

"To the Garda station," she muttered. "Somebody needs to sort out this mess."

"Ah, your granny's down there. She'll sort them all out."

But Fiona wouldn't be dissuaded. She couldn't believe that Sergeant Brennan had resorted to this. Besides, she couldn't just sit around and wait.

"Fiona—"

"No! He can't be allowed to get away with this. He's probably retaliating because of how we got involved in his last case."

Francis shrugged. "I don't see what good we'll do going down there and mouthing off at him."

Fiona refused to back down. Fury built inside her as they hurried out of the house: the thought of Sergeant Brennan harassing her poor mother!

She stormed up the road, struggling to keep pace with her older brother. Rage propelled her on. She became even more worked up when a waft of acrid smoke hit her in the face. She stopped and stared. Now that she was paying attention, she could see plumes of black smoke rising from Trish Mahony's back yard. She shook her head. What were they burning that was so toxic that the smell now clung around her face, making her feel stifled and claustrophobic?

"What the hell is that?" she growled.

Marty shrugged. "They're probably just having a bonfire."

"It doesn't smell like cut grass or tree-cuttings. It's like they're burning plastic! Why can't she use her bin like a normal person?"

"I don't know, Fi," Marty said with a sigh. "Maybe it's something personal. Like old credit cards."

"What, a whole trailer-load of them? I've a good mind to knock in there and make her smell my hair. I only washed it this morning…"

She shook her head. What did it matter what her hair smelled like? She certainly had more important things on her mind.

Marty smiled sympathetically before carrying on towards the Garda station. "Of course you're upset," he murmured. "It's understandable. You can go and give out to Trish Mahony after we've sorted this out."

They were halfway into town by the time she realised she hadn't thought to ask who her mother was supposed to have murdered.

2

"WHAT THE HELL do you think you're doing?" Fiona hissed, ignoring Garda Conway at the desk and marching into Sergeant Brennan's office. "I want my mother released now. This is harassment and I'm not afraid to go to the papers. Do you hear me?"

Brennan stared at her. He rolled his eyes and looked back at his computer monitor. "Are you sure it's a good idea to come in here and start harassing a Garda sergeant? Are you out of your mind?"

Fi baulked. That was certainly not the reaction she had expected. So much so that she struggled to think of a response. "This is ridiculous," she yelled. "My mother is nearly sixty. You can't just put her in jail to mess with us. She's done nothing wrong."

"Is that what you think?" He folded his arms and leaned them on his immaculately tidy desk.

"Of course. She wouldn't hurt a fly."

"You have to admit you're somewhat biased," he said with a sneer.

"The cheek of you," she gasped. "You won't get away with this. It's harassment pure and simple. Other people around here might be afraid to report you because of who your father is, but I'm not. You can test me on that."

He shook his head. "I can't believe you're bringing my father into this. What's he got to do with anything? I got where I am through my own abilities."

Fiona felt it was best not to respond. Instead, she shot him a look of total disbelief.

Because it was nonsense. Brennan was a bully and a bore and a whole lot of other B words that Mrs McCabe wouldn't tolerate being said in her house. Anyone else would have been fired years ago, but he was protected by his father who was a good friend of the Garda Commissioner.

His eyes narrowed. "Anyway, she's just here for questioning. At least get your facts straight."

"I'm not some Garda process nerd. I want to get my mother out of here and I'm not leaving without her."

He stared at her levelly. "I'm afraid that's not going to happen; no matter how much I'd like you out of my office and at least five hundred metres away from me."

"Believe me, I'd prefer to stay that far away from you. At least. You're making it difficult, though. She's my mother. You're harassing her. I'm not leaving without her."

He glared at her but said nothing more as he reached for the phone and hit one of the speed-dial buttons along the side.

A moment later, Garda Conway's booming voice echoed in surround sound from the phone and through the open door behind her.

"Sergeant. What can I do you for?"

Brennan winced. "I told you before not to answer the phone like that. You sound like someone out of a used car yard, not an officer of the peace."

Conway didn't respond.

The sergeant sighed. "Anyway. Can you come in here and remove Miss McCabe from my office? I have important Garda business to attend to."

"Yeah," Fiona muttered. "Like picking your nose and being a…"

Luckily, Garda Conway's laughter shook her out of her dark mood and made her stop talking before she took it too far. That was the thing about Brennan:

11

you didn't want to go too far or he'd probably charge you with breaking some obscure law nobody had heard of for several decades.

When Garda Conway lumbered in a few moments later, Fi stood and accompanied him out without arguing. She liked Conway: he'd been stationed there since she was a child and he'd always been nice to her.

"Your boss is impossible," she muttered, once they were out of earshot.

"I know," Conway said, his voice uncharacteristically low. "You should have come to me and not stormed in there. You're only winding yourself up."

"Yeah," she agreed. "But I had to go to him. He's the one who brought my mother here. What's going on, Garda Conway? How'd he set this up? He can't get away with it, surely."

At this, Conway's good-natured agreements stopped. He looked away and wouldn't meet her eyes no matter how intently she looked at him.

"What is it?" Fi asked uneasily.

"He probably tried to tell you himself, but I don't blame you for not listening. That voice would go through you."

Fiona laughed despite the situation. "It would

too. It's like a whole army of cats scraping blackboards."

"Fiona," Conway said.

There was no levity in his tone now. Her heart sank. "Level with me, Garda Conway. What's going on?"

He sighed and shook his head. "I hate to be the one to tell you this, Fiona. But your mother's being questioned in relation to the murder of Mrs May Stanley."

"May Stanley?"

"Yes. She lives on one of the lanes off the Newtownbeg road. *Used* to live."

"I know her. But I don't understand. You're telling me she's been murdered? I don't believe it."

Mrs Stanley looked the same as she'd looked back when Fiona was starting primary school. Everyone knew she was old but it was a mystery just how old she was. Fi didn't know her well but she had always seemed pleasant.

Conway nodded. "I'm afraid so. We received an anonymous tip-off about a disturbance earlier. When we arrived... well, there she was."

"And you found my mother there?"

He shook his head. "I can't really talk about the details of an open case, Fiona."

"She's my mother," she said through gritted teeth.

"You're going to need to tell us what you've got sooner or later."

"Fine. She wasn't at the scene, but she was seen in town earlier having an altercation with Mrs Stanley."

'You're joking!"

"I'm not. I'm deadly serious."

"But Mam wouldn't…" Fiona blinked. She couldn't in good conscience claim that her mother was incapable of getting into a row.

"Mam wouldn't murder anyone. And she certainly wouldn't hurt Mrs Stanley. Only a complete psychopath could murder a nice old lady."

"Well, unfortunately that's the only lead we have. It appears she was the last person to see Mrs Stanley." He shook his head and stared down at the desk.

"I can't believe you think my mother did it! Who reported her? What have you got on her exactly?"

"I can't tell you that," he said calmly. "I know you're only looking out for your mother, but I can see tempers are running high."

She sighed and bit her lip. "Okay. Fair enough. But can you tell me more about this row? As far as I know, Mam didn't really know Mrs Stanley."

Conway tapped away on his computer at the reception desk, though Fi didn't know why. It wasn't like Ballycashel was the murder capital of Ireland. It was a tiny town in the middle of nowhere, where serious crime was unheard of. Well, apart from a murder several months before. But that had been an anomaly.

Hadn't it?

Fiona gritted her teeth and told herself to stop overthinking. It was all a mistake, she suspected. Or an April Fool's joke (never mind the fact that it was September and not April). It was too crazy. It had to be a wind-up.

But Garda Conway wasn't laughing. "Ah, here we go. She was seen just hours before the victim was found, waving her handbag at Mrs Stanley and shouting and screaming."

"It must be a mistake."

"I'm afraid not," he said, shaking his head and looking genuinely sympathetic. "Not only has the account been verified by another witness, but we have video footage from one of the shops on Main Street that shows your mother clearly. There's no sound, but it's very obvious what's going on."

Fiona sighed and ran her fingers through her hair. "Can I see her? This is nuts. I need to see her and find out what's going on."

"I can't do that. The sergeant is about to go in and question her. Technically—"

"But Dad said Granny is in with her."

He groaned. "Normally I'd let you in, but I can't with the sergeant here."

Fiona was about to object but then thought better of it. She glanced at the door that led to the interview rooms and then an idea struck her. "Thanks, Garda Conway. I'll be off so."

3

FIFTEEN MINUTES LATER, Fiona and Marty watched from behind a poster in the ice-cream shop across the road as Sergeant Brennan hurried down the steps.

Grinning, she counted to ten to make sure he didn't return. When he didn't, she dumped her empty cup in the bin and hurried out.

"Hey, Garda Conway," she said breezily.

"Hello, lads. I thought you'd left."

"Ah, we thought we'd come back and try again."

Conway's eyes narrowed. "You wouldn't have anything to do with the sergeant's hurried departure now, would you?"

Fi couldn't hold back her laughter. "Oh he's gone, is he?"

The Garda couldn't hold up the pretence any

longer. "What did you do? Ha, I wouldn't put anything past you. That's comical."

"What?" she protested. "I did nothing."

"Lookit. I'm not going to tell anyone. I'm just glad to have a moment's peace. You know, he's almost fanatical about reports and checklists. Not to mention project plans. You'd swear he was responsible for keeping the peace in Beirut and not a sleepy place like Ballycashel."

Fi shrugged. "Don't know what you're talking about."

"I'll let you in to see your mammy if you tell me what you did."

She snorted. "You drive a hard bargain, Garda Conway. Sure I did nothing. But if I had to guess, I'd say he got a call about a disturbance at his house."

Garda Conway laughed and came out from behind the desk to show her into the interview room. "Just be quick, alright? The sergeant was already giving me hassle about letting in your granny. Now, I couldn't care less about him, but I'm close to retirement. A nice quiet life is all I aspire to."

"Don't we all," she grinned as she disappeared into the gloom.

"Mammy!"

Ballycashel Garda station was small; a world away from the police stations on cop shows. There was only one secure area at the back, which held both the cells and the interview rooms. There was only two of each: God alone knew what would happen if there was a spate of crime in the town. It had never happened before. As it was, the furnishings, though utilitarian, looked like they'd barely been used.

"Oh Fiona! Look what they're after doing to me!"

Fiona had to stifle the urge to laugh. Not at her mother's plight, of course, but at the setup back there. The door to her mother's interview room was wide open. All they had to do was get up and walk out of there. She noticed the door locked from the outside, but what use was that when it wasn't even shut?

"Why don't you just get up and leave?" she asked, pointing at the door.

"Ah," Granny Coyle said. "Robocop knows we wouldn't do that to Garda Conway. He'd never hear the end of it if we just sauntered out. He knows we wouldn't do that: that's why he let me in. Anyway, she's here of her own accord."

Fiona shook her head in absolute disbelief. "What happened? Garda Conway told me you were seen fighting with Mrs Stanley in the street. What on earth, Mam?"

Mrs McCabe threw back her head as if she was about to burst into a passionate defence. Her mother beat her to it.

"It's a cod," Granny Coyle declared, before folding her arms and sitting back in her chair as if to say that was the end of the matter.

It wasn't that clear-cut for Fiona. "It is, but we need to figure out a way to get out of this. I don't understand why you don't just walk out of here."

"Ah, I couldn't do that to Garda Conway. Anyway, the last thing I need is to be labelled a fugitive and hunted down like that Richard fella."

"That was a movie, Mam."

"Even so. What they did to that poor man…"

Fiona sighed and looked at Marty, who shrugged. *Very encouraging*, she thought.

"Right. We need a plan."

"Your father's working on getting me out of here and the solicitor is on his way. You shouldn't have come: this is all very embarrassing."

"What'll be more embarrassing," Fiona said through gritted teeth. "Is if you get charged and find yourself thrown in the women's prison."

"It's police harassment! I did nothing."

There was usually no talking to Mrs McCabe

when she was in such a high state of emotion, but Fiona didn't feel like she had a choice this time. "You were seen in the street fighting with Mrs Stanley," she said as gently as she could. "It sounds like that's their whole reasoning for arresting you. What was that about? I thought you barely knew her?"

Mrs McCabe remained silent, which was unusual for her.

"Come on, Mam. Just tell me. Stop being so stubborn." Fi clamped her mouth shut, realising too late that she'd said exactly the wrong thing.

"Stubborn?" her mother snapped. "Stubborn? You have the cheek to call me stubborn? None of ye get to do that after the heartbreak you put me through when you were small. Do you remember that time you refused to go to school and you couldn't be tempted in there for love nor money? Two weeks you lasted. And I mortified beyond belief."

Fi nodded, knowing it was best if she just stayed quiet. Once Mrs McCabe started reminiscing it could go on for hours.

"Actually, I think money was what resolved it in the end," Marty said, deadpan.

Fiona remembered it well. Well, she had a clear memory of the pound coin she'd been bribed with. Looking back on it, she thought she'd let them off lightly and she should have gone higher and demanded at least a fiver.

"Mammy," she whispered. "You can call me stubborn all you like. But let's get you out of here first, okay?"

Mrs McCabe pursed her lips. She nodded her head almost imperceptibly.

"Right," Fi said. "What were you doing fighting on the street with Mrs Stanley?"

"I wasn't fighting."

"Well what were you doing?" Fiona took great care to keep her voice gentle. She didn't want to risk setting her mother off again and it was only a matter of time before Sergeant Brennan realised it was a hoax and made his way back to the station. "They have you on video, apparently."

Her mother sighed. "It's all a big misunderstanding."

"What were you doing? According to their witnesses, you were waving your handbag around and yelling blue murder. What could have made you so mad at Mrs Stanley?"

"It's a long story." She made no attempt to clarify.

"I see," Fi said, glancing behind her at the door. Several minutes had passed now. Robocop would be back at any moment. The pressure was beginning to get to her, she realised. "Why don't you tell me?"

"You wouldn't understand."

"Try me."

"What's the point?"

"Thanks for the vote of confidence," Fiona sniffed.

Granny Coyle glared at her daughter and granddaughter in turn. "You're as bad as each other," she muttered. "I'll tell you what happened."

Before she could speak, though, the door flew open.

4

"WHAT ON EARTH is going on here?" Sergeant Brennan cried. "I was sceptical enough letting one of you in and now you seem to have multiplied!"

"I can't believe you used to go out with him, Fiona," Mrs McCabe muttered, glaring at the sergeant with undisguised loathing.

Granny Coyle's eyes widened to the size of saucers. "Tell me she's making that up, love. Sure you can't stand the sight of him. Don't you lament the day he ever set foot in this place?"

Fiona shrugged. "It was supposed to be a secret. Anyway, we never went out. It was just one bad date. Mam is exaggerating as usual."

"I'm standing right here!" Sergeant Brennan bellowed.

"More's the pity."

The sergeant rounded on Granny Coyle. "I'd expect that from this lot, but not from you, Mrs Coyle."

At this, she threw her head back and laughed heartily. Her grandchildren were all fascinated by the fact that such a petite old lady who looked like a picture postcard version of a grandmother could have the filthy laugh of an errant sailor. But that was Rose Coyle: full of surprises.

The smile vanished from her face. "Don't you judge me, Brennan. Now, you'll leave us be if you know what's good for you."

"Is that a threat, Mrs Coyle? Because if it is I have to warn you—"

"A threat?" she spat. "You're accusing an old age pensioner of threatening you? Good God Almighty. Have you nothing better to do?"

He flushed. "I can't have you all back here."

"Well, we're staying," Rose said firmly. "So you had better skedaddle back out there and get back to whatever it is you do on that computer of yours. Drawing pictures most likely. Go on."

"You can't speak to me like that!"

Granny Coyle smiled. "What are you going to do, arrest me too? Is that your game? You want to have a full collection of us?"

"Mammy." Mrs McCabe's embarrassment was unmistakeable. "Maybe you should…"

"I'll do nothing, Margaret. I'll tell you what I'll do. I'll stay here at least until that solicitor comes. And then I'll see if he's any good. If he is I'll leave you with him and get over to make the dinner for Francis and the kids. If not… well, I'll defend you myself if I have to."

Mrs McCabe sighed. It usually amused Fiona to see her mother put in her place by her grandmother, but this time it gave her no satisfaction.

"Give us a few minutes, Sergeant, would you?"

He groaned, but then he turned and left, clearly defeated. Granny Coyle's laughter rang out before the door had even closed.

"I never thought I'd say this to anyone about Brennan," Fiona hissed to her grandmother. "But maybe you shouldn't wind him up like that. We want to get Mam out of this, don't we?"

"That's debatable," her grandmother said, arching her perfectly-plucked brows. "From what I've heard, Margaret here is responsible for telling the parish council tales on me."

"I only did it because you're out of control, Mammy."

Granny Coyle baulked. "Out of control, my eye. Anyway, even if I was out of control, you shouldn't have gone squealing to them. Have you never heard of omerta?"

"Om…" Mrs McCabe started to say.

Fiona sighed and massaged her temples. "You're not a mafia don, Granny. Or a donna or whatever the female version is. Listen, we don't have long. I'm amazed Brennan even left us back here the way he did."

"It's because ye annoyed the head off him," Marty observed. "What did Mam report you for, Granny?"

"Not now!" Fiona hissed. "Okay Mam, listen. You've got to focus and tell me what happened. I'm not sure I should tell you this, but Dad has gone to pieces. He's not going to be of any help to you. If you tell me what's going on, I'll coordinate the others. We'll do everything we can to get you out of this."

Margaret McCabe's eyes grew watery. "Thank you, Fiona."

"You just need to tell me what happened with Mrs Stanley."

Her mother closed up again in an instant.

"Just come on. What could be so bad? What's better, tell me now or keep quiet and have us read about it in the paper."

On hearing that, Mrs McCabe seemed to shrink into herself. "No, not the papers. Please. It's bad

27

enough thinking that all the neighbours know I'm down here. You can't tell the papers."

"I'm not going to tell the papers," Fiona said, rolling her eyes. "But it'll get out eventually. You know what people are like around here. I bet we'll have Simon Moriarty down here looking to do a true crime documentary on you."

Mrs McCabe's face went all dreamy for a moment, betraying her soft spot for the journalist. He was something of a heartthrob to middle aged women all over Ireland. Fiona wished she hadn't mentioned his name, but she hadn't been thinking straight. She'd been too busy trying to talk some sense into her mother.

"Come on, Mam. It was a stupid thing for me to say. You really think you have a chance with him after the stunt you pulled, tricking him into—?"

"I thought you were trying to sort this out, Fi."

Fiona rolled her eyes at her brother. "It's impossible to stay on-topic in this family. You should know that." She turned to her mother. "But he's right. You need to tell us what happened on the street. Now."

"It's embarrassing."

"So? You're always doing embarrassing stuff."

"Stop it, Marty. Don't give her an excuse to change the subject again."

"But you're the one who—"

"Would ye both just—"

"Alright!" Mrs McCabe yelled. "I'll tell ye. But you have to promise not to laugh."

Fiona nodded eagerly. "I promise." She didn't mean a bar of it, of course, but she'd say anything to get to the truth.

"Martin?"

Marty nodded, his face contorted into a smirk that suggested he didn't mean it either.

"Mammy?"

"Oh fine so, if that's what you want to hear."

"It's not what I want to hear. I want you to promise not to mock me when I tell you."

"I promise," Rose Coyle said sweetly. Fiona noticed she'd crossed the fingers of her left hand as she said it.

"Fine," Mrs McCabe huffed, glancing anxiously at the door and lowering her voice. "Shut that door and come in. I don't want anyone else to hear."

"Just tell us. I don't want to close the door. What if Brennan comes and locks us in?"

"Fine. Okay. I suppose it'll spread like wildfire anyway knowing this place. Oh my, it's so embarrassing."

They all watched her, undisguised anticipation written all over their eager faces.

"She was on that Facebook and she had a picture of me on it. You know, the one they had done up for the parish council page."

Fiona sat back heavily in her chair. The plastic creaked. The chairs were identical to the ones they'd had in primary school: moulded plastic on shaky metal legs. "Why would she have your picture? Maybe she was just looking at the parish page?"

She looked around. The others looked similarly bewildered.

"No. She was using it."

"But why would she do that? Does she even have the internet? Mam, I'm seriously worried about you right now. Are you sure you haven't been smoking something?"

"Quite sure, Fiona. I have never touched a cigarette and I never intend to. I pride myself on that."

"She wasn't talking about—"

"Mam, I don't get it. Why would you get so worked up about her just looking at a picture of you?"

"I don't know," Mrs McCabe admitted. "It was strange. I can't explain it. It was the way she reacted. I got a fright and called out to her and the next thing she was looking at me like she'd been caught in the act! She was up and out of that chair before I had a chance to get over to her."

Fiona was alarmed by the amount of bile in her mother's words. "She's a sweet old lady."

That, apparently, was exactly the wrong thing to say.

"She is in my eye," Mrs McCabe spat. "She's a little monster."

"That's what you were fighting about? She looked at a picture of you?"

Mrs McCabe shook her head. "Didn't I tell you it wasn't the... Ah, it was just strange. I got curious then so I chased her out of the library and caught up with her on Main Street."

"How did you end up shouting and roaring at her? It's not a crime to look at pictures on the internet."

Mrs McCabe wrinkled her nose as if a bad smell had just wafted into the room. "She couldn't explain it! That was the odd thing. Not only that, but she had the cheek to get all shifty with me then. As if I was the one in the wrong for catching her in the act!"

Fiona exhaled loudly and looked at the others. They appeared equally confused.

"So what happened then?"

"Well I gave her a piece of my mind! Told her it wasn't right to run off like that; that she could have just told me what she was at. Oh, I suspected it, see. There was only one reason for her to be on that parish site. I'd bet you good money that she's after my seat on the council. And she not lifting a finger to help out around the place!"

"Wait now. Did she admit to any of this?"

"No, she did not," Mrs McCabe huffed, growing more indignant by the minute. "Not even when I threatened to grab her by the scruff of the neck and drag her to see Father Jimmy!"

Fiona covered her face with her hands. "Please tell me you didn't—"

"Oh, of course I didn't! How would that have looked? She knew well I couldn't do anything, the sneaky little beggar."

"So what did you do?"

"I went home, Fiona. What else could I do? I had to get back and call the others on the council to find out if she'd been badmouthing me."

"Mammy," Marty said slowly. "There's something else I don't quite get. What's so embarrassing about this?"

"Surely I don't have to tell you that! The cheek of her! Driving me to confrontation in the street!"

"Okay, okay, Mam," Fiona said, trying to get the situation under control again. "Let's ignore the fact that she provoked you. What happened after that?"

"I told you. I went home to call the other members of the council and see if they'd heard anything about her trying to muscle in."

"And after that?"

Mrs McCabe looked affronted. "You think I did it, don't you?!"

Fiona shook her head. "I just hope you didn't, but from the sounds of it, you had a pretty heated argument just before she was killed."

"Oh Fiona!" her mother threw her hands up. "I went home and rang around. It crossed my mind to go over there and try to get the truth out of her, but I didn't. I got the dinner on instead because I knew there was no point in bothering. She's too sly."

"I don't get it. If you were home, why can't Dad or Ben just come down here and tell them that?"

"That's the thing, Fiona," Margaret said, looking hunted. "Usually there'd be somebody around the house, but everyone was out this morning. I was home alone until half an hour before the guards came. Nobody can vouch for me to say I didn't go over to Mrs Stanley's."

5

"Right," Fiona said, marching into the sitting room and plugging out the telly. "We need to sit down and try to get to the bottom of this."

"Ah, what? I was watching that," Ben groaned.

Fiona stood in front of the screen even though there was no way he could see anything on it. "If Mam heard you say a thing like that…"

"Well she can't, can she? She's in jail."

"She's not in jail," Francis said. "She's in the station for questioning. There's a difference."

"Yeah, and that difference is mainly timing. They need to charge her soon or else release her."

"There you go, so," Ben said. "We can get back to watching the match and we'll see her tomorrow."

"You've changed your tune since earlier.

Remember? You rang me and you were almost in tears. What happened?"

"I think Spurs scored is what happened," their father said drily.

Ben shrugged. "So? I've been looking forward to this match for ages."

"You're her favourite," Fiona snapped. "She'd be devastated if she knew you didn't care about clearing her name. Right, everyone else: come and help. We've got to get to the bottom of this."

"Ah, Fiona," her father groaned. "It's all a bit far-fetched, isn't it? I mean, I'd be worried if they were holding her for disturbing the peace, but murder? No. It'll never stick."

"What are you talking about Dad? They wouldn't have her down there if they didn't think she could be done for it. Why are you burying your head in the sand?"

Far from being convinced, though, he just seemed irritated. He waved her away as if she was a fly buzzing around his head. "Plug in the television there Ben, there's a good lad."

"LOOKS like it's just us two then."

Marty nodded. "Looks like it. Ah, Granny

probably would have helped but she's staying with Mam. Brennan's trying to intimidate her by questioning her overnight."

"That man is unbelievable," she said, shuddering. "Anyway, there's not a lot we can do about that. How do we clear her name? How do we get Mam out? Am I the only one who sees this as serious? They all think it's a joke, but you heard her earlier. She was absolutely raging at Mrs Stanley. All Robocop needs to do is hear that and I bet he'll throw the book at her."

"They don't have any evidence, though."

"Do they need it? You heard her. She was caught on camera arguing with the woman just a few hours before she wound up dead. Then she went home but there's nobody to prove that."

"You don't think she did it, do you?"

"Of course not," Fiona said without hesitation. "But it's not me we need to convince: it's Brennan."

"I know. It's hopeless, isn't it?"

Fiona shook her head. "It can't be. Dad's in shock and Mam isn't far off. Brennan is convinced it's her. We've got to prove it wasn't."

"How do we prove she was here? Nobody else was around."

"I don't know."

They lapsed into silence then, both staring down

at their hands. After several minutes of this, Marty shook his head.

"We're in trouble, aren't we?"

"I'd say so," Fiona said gravely. "How are we supposed to clear her name if we don't have any idea what happened?"

He shook his head.

That was the thing. They knew Mrs Stanley had been poisoned in her own home, sometime in the late morning. That was it. They didn't know anything about the woman, much less about who she associated with or any enemies she might have had.

"Maybe Dad knows something."

"No," Fi said with a sigh. "And even if he did he's in no state to tell us. I've never seen him like this, Marty. He's beside himself. We've got to find the real killer."

Marty looked thoughtful.

"What is it?"

"I don't know," he said slowly, staring off into space. "I don't know anything about Mrs Stanley. Nothing at all. How many people in town can you say that about?"

Fiona shook her head. "Not many. But it doesn't prove a thing. Maybe she was just quiet."

"That's it. She kept herself to herself. So what did she do that made somebody want to kill her?"

"Money?"

"She didn't have any. Unless she had a secret stash that nobody knew about."

Fi shook her head. "No, I remember something Granny Coyle said now. Granny never liked her much. Said she used to go visit her sister in Florida every year. She stopped doing it a few years ago. Granny was giving out; wishing Mrs Stanley would take her grumpy head off to Florida and spare Granny the sight of her."

Marty buried his head in his hands. "So Granny had a real beef with her. How's that going to look?"

"It's not as if Mam killed the woman on Granny Coyle's behalf now, is it? I wasn't saying that; just that it's unlikely she was murdered for her money."

"What then?"

"Come on."

Fiona stood and followed him to the door. "Where? Where are you going at this hour? It's not like she's got any family in the area we can talk to."

He grinned. "Who said we were going to talk to anybody?"

6

"I DON'T LIKE THIS," Fi protested as they walked along the dark road.

"I didn't force you to come with me," Marty called back cheerfully.

She hadn't had to ask where he intended to go: she'd understood from the look in his eyes. Marty had always loved doing things he wasn't supposed to, but this took the cake.

"Because I'm not leaving you alone."

"Stop moaning so."

"I'm not moaning," she hissed, treading carefully to avoid slipping on the muddy verge. "I'm just scared. We could get in a lot of trouble if we're caught."

His laughter was startling in the still air. "Who's

going to catch us? Brennan is down at the station trying to drive Mam to distraction. Conway is down at Phelan's."

"We could head down there. Try and find out what he knows."

"I swung by Phelan's after I closed up the shop this evening. I could tell from the way he was talking that he knew nothing. The others were lapping it up, of course. If these murders keep up, Conway will be a celebrity around these parts."

"They won't keep up," Fiona hissed, shivering despite the mild evening. "Don't say a thing like that."

"I was only passing comment. That's all."

"I know," she whispered, rushing forward to keep up with him despite the uneven ground. "I'm just a little creeped out by this."

"You're a wuss."

"I'll gladly admit to that. Can we go home now?"

"No. I'm certain there's something in that house that'll clear Mam's name."

"The guards will find it if it's there."

He stopped abruptly and she almost collided with him. "Are you serious? You're the first one around here who'll talk about how incompetent the Ballycashel Gardaí are. And you want to trust your mother's freedom to that shower?"

"No, but…"

"Well then, stop. Do you see the sense in what I'm saying?"

She nodded in the darkness. "Yeah," she said. "They'd need a map to find their own heads. Conway is lovely but he'd be a better granddad than a detective."

"Come on, so. Unless you want to go home."

"I'm not leaving you."

"Good. I'm glad to hear it. There's something very creepy about going into a murder scene. Let's hope her ghost is well gone."

"Marty!"

"Sorry," he said, snorting with laughter. "I thought you didn't believe in that sort of stuff."

"That's not to say I won't be creeped out by it when we're sneaking around in the middle of the night."

"Don't worry. I'll protect you."

"Hmm."

Fiona focussed on her breathing, telling herself there was nothing to worry about. It had taken a while, but her eyes finally started to adjust to the darkness. There were no street lights this far outside of the centre of the town.

She frowned as she noticed a darker patch than the rest up ahead and was startled when she realised it was someone coming towards them. She must have jumped from fright.

"Whoa, you're skittish."

"Sorry," she said sheepishly. "I guess I creeped myself out thinking about getting caught and that."

"Don't worry. We're doing nothing wrong; just going for a walk."

"I know," she whispered, telling herself to calm down and not let on how jumpy she was.

As it turned out, though, it wasn't a friend of theirs. It was Jimmy Brady. He had always been a quiet man, but he'd become even more withdrawn in recent months. Someone had distributed anonymous flyers around town revealing that he'd applied to have wind turbines built on his land. It was a contentious enough issue around town as it was, but it was made more devastating in Jimmy Brady's case because he'd been publicly opposed to the turbines.

"Poor man," Marty muttered, when they'd passed the mournful-looking old farmer.

Fiona sighed. "What he did was a bit underhand, but the way he's been outcast is just vicious."

They walked on in silence, each lost in their own thoughts. Fi knew Marty was right and if he hadn't insisted on going to Mrs Stanley's house, she would probably have come up with the idea on her own. She was glad that she didn't have to go in there alone, but the thought of creeping around in the dark wasn't very appealing.

"Won't we see more if we wait until it's bright?"

"I brought a torch."

"But you won't be able to use it. What if someone sees?"

"They won't. The curtains are probably drawn just like they always are. Nobody'll be close enough to see torchlight."

"What if the guards are keeping watch?"

"They won't be. I told you. Conway is in Phelan's for the night and Fitzpatrick has his hands full with a house full of kids. Brennan is probably hiding out in his office and licking his wounds from the hard time Granny is giving him."

"True." She was running out of objections.

"Here we are," Marty said cheerily. It was completely dark now, but they'd held off from using the torch in case anyone spotted them walking past. They knew from experience that the residents of Ballycashel often had little better to do than stare out their windows and wait for one of the McCabes to do something remarkable or gossip-worthy.

"How are we going to get in?" She whispered as they walked up the path as quietly as they could.

"Aha," Marty said. "Well I'm hoping there's a spare key."

"Oh," Fi said, disappointed. "Isn't that hoping for a bit too much?"

He shrugged as they reached the front door and started checking under the flower pots.

Fiona was amazed when they found two keys underneath a pot beside the back door. She was even more amazed when they fit in the lock.

"See," Marty whispered, closing the door noiselessly behind them. "Most people keep spare keys around the place. I tell them not when they come in to get them cut, but I know they don't listen."

Fi sighed. "I guess it's a good thing for us that they don't. If we'd been looking for an open window we'd have been out of luck."

"Yeah. It doesn't seem like there's been a window open here for quite some time. I'll just run through and check all the curtains are closed before we risk using the torch."

He took off, but within a few steps he stopped abruptly after nearly tripping over a pile of crockery in the middle of the kitchen floor.

"Whoa," he whistled. "Whoever broke in here was certainly thorough."

Fiona looked around. Now that her eyes had adjusted to the darkness of the inside of the house, she could see that the floor was completely covered and that the drawers and kitchen presses had been completely emptied out.

Marty moved carefully to the door and closed it before switching on his torch. Fiona foolishly expected the beam of light to immediately land on something that identified the murderer, but there was nothing.

"It's just plates. Teapots."

Everything was in pieces on the floor. The thief hadn't left any stone untouched: a bag of porridge had been tipped out onto the floor. The table was the only clear surface in the room—the guards must have taken everything that was on it as evidence.

Fiona shivered at the thought.

"Be careful not to touch anything," she said, as they moved to the door and Marty switched off the torch. "Or if you do, make sure to cover your hand with your sleeve."

They tiptoed along the short hall to the sitting room.

"Good God," Marty whispered, as his foot crunched on something that sounded like broken glass. "They even pulled the pictures off the walls."

"It was so obviously a burglary gone wrong," Fi muttered. "Why would the guards even think Mam did it?"

Marty didn't reply. He made his way carefully

across the room and pulled the curtains so there were no gaps between them that might allow their torchlight to be seen. He clicked on the torch.

"Whoa."

"What?"

"Look."

Fiona followed the beam of the torch and gasped. She certainly hadn't expected to see a state-of-the art flat-screen television on the wall and that wasn't because she begrudged an old woman her creature comforts.

Mrs Stanley wasn't supposed to have two pennies to rub together. Stranger still, why would any burglar worth his salt leave such an expensive TV just hanging on the wall?

"Maybe he didn't see it," Fiona said without much conviction.

"Well he didn't miss this." Marty patted the top of an all-in-one computer unit. "This model was only released about six months ago."

Fiona stepped carefully over the mess to get a closer look. It soon became clear to her that the burglar certainly hadn't missed the computer: it was smashed.

"Why wouldn't he just steal it instead of destroying it? This is getting weirder and weirder. Mam said she saw Mrs Stanley on one of the library computers. Why would she use those when she has her own fancy computer?"

"Maybe she smashed it herself."

"Why would she do that?"

"I don't know," Marty sighed, moving to the sideboard. The doors were open and the contents of the drawers had been tipped on the ground. He paused. "This feels wrong."

"I know. It's horrible. But if I had to choose between doing this and seeing Mam go to prison…"

He started rummaging in the pile without saying another word. Fiona went to his side and took the torch from him, holding it up so he could see what he was looking at. The sight didn't fill her with hope. The floor was covered with envelopes of all different shapes and sizes.

After a few minutes, Marty sighed. "This is hopeless. If there's anything useful in here, there's no way we're going to find it among all these bills and letters. Plus the thief probably took anything valuable."

"Wait a sec," Fiona said, reaching past him. "What's this?"

The blue plastic envelope hadn't been visible until Marty had flipped over the last envelope, but now it was unmissable. Fi pulled it out and looked at it. The logo was instantly recognisable: they walked past

Ann's Travel Services every time they went into town.

Fiona's gut told her what she was going to see before her shaking fingers had even managed to pull open the flap.

Sure enough, it was a ticket to Fort Lauderdale, via Orlando, dated two weeks in the future.

"What's going on, Marty? Do you think she did a really good job of fooling us all? With that computer and telly and now these flights—she's definitely not broke! Maybe money was the motive after all."

He shook his head, obviously as confused as she was. "She wasn't broke, but whoever murdered her can't have been after her money. If they were then they're eejits. Even if they did get cash, why not take the telly and computer?"

Fiona shook her head. "Maybe there was so much cash they didn't feel the need to come back?"

"Or maybe," Marty said, with a voice that made his sister shiver. "They didn't have the transportation that day. It was broad daylight after all."

"I don't like it," Fiona said with a shudder.

"It's grand," her brother said, starting to flick through the envelopes again. "They obviously didn't want the computer if they smashed it like that. Only a complete fool would come back here when the guards are still treating it as a crime scene."

"Like we just did?"

"No!" he exclaimed. "We have a very good reason for being here. Aren't... Wait a second. What's this?"

He pulled out an envelope with a logo on it that Fiona didn't recognise at first. Something about it must have resonated with Marty, though, because his fingers shook as he pulled the letter from the already open envelope.

"Look at this!" he said, after he'd skimmed over the first few lines. "It's a letter from the wind farm people. This is saying that they've chosen her site out on the Cloher road for the development of two turbines! This explains everything, Fi! The money, the reason someone hated her so much that they could kill her! Remember the bile that old Brady faced and that was before he even got approval!"

"You think someone would kill her over a wind turbine?"

He nodded eagerly as if the answer was obvious. "Yeah, I wouldn't doubt it for a second. You've seen how up in arms people got over them. Look at all the posters that are still up on power poles. People really don't want them around. I don't mind them, but then I suppose we're far enough away from the proposed sites that they wouldn't bother any of us."

Fiona shuddered. It seemed like they had their answer. Mrs Stanley had gotten a payout from the turbine company and booked a flight hoping she could escape off to the US before anyone found out. It looked like someone had got wind of it before she could get away. Now all they needed to do was figure out which of Mrs Stanley's neighbours had taken the law into their own hands.

"Come on," she whispered, no longer able to stand being in poor Mrs Stanley's house.

"But we've still got all the other rooms to check."

"Please. It's creeping me out. I think we've found out enough."

"Okay," Marty said. "Come on."

They snuck back through the quiet house and let themselves out. Fiona began to relax once they reached the path. She was about to suggest they stop off to get fish and chips when she was suddenly thrown off balance and into the hedge. She opened her mouth to scream but someone clamped their hand over it before she could do so.

7

"IT's OKAY, it's okay, it's okay. That was me," Marty whispered in her ear, slowly removing his hand.

"What the hell was that? She hissed, falling silent when she saw he'd clamped his index finger to his lips.

He shook his head. From the little light the moon was casting on his face she could see he looked worried. Haunted even. She shivered.

"Someone's coming." His voice was barely a whisper.

"Who?" she asked, her heart starting to race.

"I don't know. I saw a flash of torchlight. It can't have been headlights: it wasn't strong enough. Did I hurt you? I panicked and did the first thing that came into my head."

"I didn't know it was you. I thought somebody else had—"

"Shh."

A beam of torch light had just lit up the path to the house. Fiona felt as if her heart was going to burst out of her chest, it was beating so hard. Who was creeping around here in the middle of the night? It was past nine. Okay fair enough, it wasn't exactly late. But it was dark.

Brennan, she thought. She looked around and was relieved to see they were completely hidden from view by the boxy hedge. They'd be in trouble if anyone left the path and came behind the hedge, but she could see no reason for the intruder to do that.

A thought gripped her. Why would Brennan leave an interview he clearly relished and then go to the trouble of walking here if he could have taken his squad car? There was no need for him to go sneaking about.

Unless...

Fiona blinked and told herself to get a grip. It was hard to do that, though, when you were crouched behind a hedge at a murder scene. How had she allowed Marty to convince her that this was a good idea?

She bit the insides of her cheeks. The beam was getting brighter. She didn't like the way it bounced up and down. It was too jerky; too fast. This was somebody walking with intent, not out for a casual walk. Probably not the kind of person you wanted to meet in the middle of the night.

She gripped Marty's arm so hard that he winced.

"Sorry," she mouthed.

He shook his head, beyond frustrated.

Before she could do anything else, a pair of legs moved past them. She wasn't sure what colour they were in the dim moonlight and the torch was shining in the opposite direction. She realised with a sinking heart that they were so low down that they didn't have a hope of seeing the person's face.

Focus, Fiona, she told herself.

Big shoes. Sturdy.

Most likely a man.

Jeans?

She listened and heard the tell-tale swish. Yes, jeans.

She stared at his ankles. These weren't the skinny jeans that young guys wore or the baggy shapeless type worn by older men.

And then she realised. They weren't jeans at all, but chinos.

She shook her head in disbelief, but knew she hadn't been mistaken. But who wore chinos in Ballycashel? Could it be Jimmy Brady? After all, it was possible the killer had bought clothes in order to disguise himself. But he'd been wearing tattered old jeans and a filthy coat when they had passed him on the road.

She heard a rustling sound and a muttered curse that startled her and made her jump. Luckily the mystery man seemed more focussed on whatever had caused him to cry out than on listening out for strange women hidden in the bushes.

He swore again and kicked something.

The key! Fiona realised. They'd left on the hall table! She had intended to replace it under the flowerpot when they left, but she'd completely forgotten!

She glanced at Marty and knew from his panic-stricken face that he had realised the same thing. What if the killer knew about the spare key and came looking for it?

There was the sound of a muttered curse and a moment later, the sound of glass breaking filled the still country air. Fiona was rigid with fear now. What was going to happen next? Who had the cheek to break into a house that was central to a murder investigation? The guards would be back the following morning! He must know that!

The shuffling sound stopped or became too faint for them to hear. Fiona crept forward on her hands and knees, craning her neck to get a glimpse of the front door. The man had disappeared, but she didn't know if he'd gone through the window or gone around the back. It was too dark to see which window had been broken.

Marty crept alongside her and she shook her head and pushed him back. "He might see you," she hissed. "You need to get back to the hedge."

"Come on, Fi. It's time to get out of here."

She shook her head. "No. We need to find out who it is."

"It doesn't matter."

"Yes it does," she said, retreating backwards so they weren't so close to the house. "Don't you see? That's probably the murderer."

"I can't think of a better reason to leave. Can you?"

She nodded and they hurried back towards the gate, bursting through the hedge at the end of the path. Even though there was no torchlight visible, it was still nerve-wracking to think that that guy could be standing there waiting for them.

But he wasn't. They hurried out the gate and crouched behind the stone wall, moving as quickly as they could to get away from the house.

"I have an idea," Fiona whispered when they

were far enough away. "Where did you see the torch come from?"

"This way," he whispered. "Definitely this way."

She nodded. There were only two ways to approach the house. It would take more than an hour to loop back around the other side of the lane, which came out further along the Newtownbeg road: it wouldn't make sense to come in one way and out the other, especially on foot.

Fi grabbed Marty's arm and gestured across the narrow road. It was another stone wall, but she knew from memory that it wasn't as sturdy as it looked. In fact, it was ideal.

Marty groaned but it was obvious that he was just as keen to find out who that man was. Fi glanced behind them. There was no sign of torchlight. She was thankful that both of them were dressed in dark colours and that she hadn't changed into her running clothes, with their reflective strips that would have shone in the killer's torchlight and made her a target.

They hurried along and through the open gate of the abandoned house. Then they doubled back along the wall, stepping high to get through the tall grass in the overgrown garden.

"I don't even want to know what I'm stepping on," Marty whispered.

"It doesn't matter. We might be able to catch a glimpse of his face from here."

"How? It's a wall, Fiona. You can't see through them and it's taller than me."

"Shhh. He might be coming. Look." She stopped and positioned herself in front of a large crack where some of the cement had crumbled away. Marty did the same at another spot close by. A few moments later he let out a quiet sigh. "I can't see anything."

She leaned over and whispered in his ear. "Trust me. All we need is the glow from his torch. It's worth a shot."

They waited and waited. Fi shifted from foot to foot, her legs itching ever since Marty had mentioned the unidentified nasties that might have been lurking in the long grass. She tried not to think about it, reasoning that she'd have a nice long bath as soon as she got home.

Soon, she started to yawn. She hadn't eaten all day and hunger was beginning to gnaw at her, though thankfully her stomach remained silent for now. Then the cold began to bite. It had been nice and warm earlier, but now it was dark it was damp and chilly. There wasn't a cloud in the sky to keep the heat in. She'd be thankful for that tomorrow, but right then she could have used some warmth.

And then the light flashed. Fiona held her breath.

Because she only had a partial field of vision thanks to the wall, she couldn't tell how far away the man was. All she knew was he was out there somewhere with his flashlight. She reached over slowly and tapped Marty's arm. He nodded.

It felt like hours passed before the torch beam grew stronger. Then she heard the footsteps; the regular creak of leather shoes. She made a mental note of that: the suspect wore leather shoes and chinos. She blinked, trying to commit it to memory.

When she opened her eyes, though, she found she no longer needed a description of what the suspect was wearing.

Her eyes widened. She only got a brief glimpse of him as he walked past, but she had no doubt in her mind.

It was Alan Power.

Alan Power had broken into Mrs Stanley's house. And judging from the awkward angle of his elbow, he hadn't left empty handed.

8

THEY WAITED behind the wall for a long time. It felt like hours, but neither one was willing to suggest leaving. Fiona wanted to be absolutely sure the man was gone.

Eventually, she tapped Marty on the arm. It had been quiet for several minutes. Alan Power would need to be incredibly paranoid to still be lurking around, and he'd have no reason to think they were watching him: if they saw him they could just say they were visiting Ben's friend Barry who lived up the road.

"Did you see that?" she whispered as softly as she could.

"I know," Marty muttered. "I can't believe it was Power."

She shook her head. She didn't know Alan Power well. He was another one of the commuter brigade, with the only difference being that he had bought a terraced house in the town rather than a house in one of the new developments on the outskirts.

"Did you see? It looked like he had something big under his arm. I couldn't make out what it was."

"I don't know what it was either. It looked like a big box maybe? Something awkward to carry."

She sighed. "Money, maybe? But we didn't see any. He wasn't in there for very long so it can't have been well hidden. It must have been in one of the other rooms!"

"Come on, Fi. Let's go home."

She bit her lip. "What if we were wrong? What if it's not about the wind turbines at all? We need to go back there."

"To see what? We're not going to find what he took; not if it was from one of the rooms we didn't check."

She sighed. "Then we have to go to his house. If we hurry and cut through the fields up here we might beat him to it."

Marty groaned. "Are you actually serious? That's the stupidest thing I've ever heard you suggest, and I was there for your teenage years, remember? You're talking about confronting a murderer!"

"What other choice do we have? Anyway there are two of us."

"No. I'm not going there, especially not with my little sister."

"Don't be silly. This is an emergency."

"We're not going to confront him, Fi! Are you mad?"

"It's the only thing we can do to help Mam. We need to know what he took. Just say we tell the guards anonymously—they'll get out there tomorrow morning at the very earliest and by that stage Power could have all the evidence destroyed. He might even have vanished off to Spain or somewhere with the cash."

"We're *not* confronting him. Anyway, who said it was cash?"

"I'm assuming here. What else could it be? He was hardly after her knickers."

"Ah Jesus, thanks a lot for that mental image."

She grinned, even though she knew he wouldn't be able to see the expression on her face. Marty pretended he was tough, but she knew from experience he was one of the most squeamish people she had ever come across.

"Don't," he warned. "I know you. Stop trying to wind me up."

She opened her mouth to do just that, but froze before she could get the words out.

It had been the merest flash; only a second or two at most, but she had definitely seen it.

9

"MARTY," she whispered as quietly as she could. "Did you see that?"

He groaned. "What now? Why do I get the feeling this is part of an elaborate windup?"

"No! Listen! I saw something! A light going past that gap in the wall."

He exhaled sharply. "It was probably a car."

She accepted this for a moment before it dawned on her that it couldn't have been. "It wasn't. We would have heard it. No, I saw a flash of light go past. I'm sure of it."

He sighed. "Maybe it was Brady coming back. Or it could have been Barry cycling past."

"Yeah, but..." she sighed and trying to calm herself. It made sense. Of course it made sense that it was just one of the locals walking by. But the other explanation niggled at her. What if it was Power, back to finish them off? She suggested as much to Marty.

"Why? What would be the point in it?"

She knew he was right, even if she couldn't make herself see sense. "Come on. Let's go back to Mam and Dad's. I could use a cuppa before I head back to the flat."

"Are you going to be alright staying there on your own tonight? Maybe you should stay at the parents'. They're always delighted to have any of us stay." He groaned. It wasn't like a normal night where they could go home and find a dinner waiting for them as if their mother knew they were on their way without them even saying it.

"Maybe I should stay anyway. It must be awful for poor Dad being in the place by himself."

"Doesn't he have Ben and Kate there with him?"

She rolled her eyes. "What use are those two in a crisis? You should have heard Ben on the phone to me when he rang to say Mam was arrested. He was freaking out. For one brief moment I thought he might have grown up a bit. But no, this evening his normal priorities have returned. It's all about the football and he's just helping Dad to bury his head in the sand. And as for Kate? I don't even know where she is."

"It doesn't matter. All we need is Dad. We can come up with a plan to get this information to the guards. It's the only way, Fi. Someone is out here. Let's just get home to where it's safe."

"STUPID," Francis McCabe groaned. "What on earth were you thinking? You don't go around breaking into people's houses. We didn't raise you to do things like that."

"We didn't break in," Fi said. "We found the key."

"Oh wonderful," her father said, casting his eyes towards the ceiling in the perfectly exaggerated motion he'd perfected years ago. "That fills me with relief. You didn't break in. You went wandering around a dead woman's house but it's all grand, because you happened to find a key. Jesus, Mary and Joseph, this debacle just keeps getting more and more ridiculous as the day goes on. What next?"

"Dad, listen. We're not telling you this for the craic. Just listen, would you? We found nothing in the house, but as we were leaving, Marty saw something. We hid just in time. The next thing we knew, Alan

Power was walking up the path and breaking a window to get into the place."

Francis McCabe's expression transformed within seconds. "What are you saying?"

She shrugged. "I don't know. Doesn't it speak for itself? We got away and hid behind the wall of the old Miller house—this was before we knew it was Alan Power. He came past us a while later, carrying a box under his arm. We think it was filled with cash."

"But Mrs Stanley is broke. Everyone knows that."

"Well then explain to me what was in that box he was willing to break into a crime scene to get. We didn't see a box just sitting around on the table, so it's something he knew about. Maybe he'd been scoping the place out earlier and she surprised him."

"Maybe. It still doesn't sound right to me," Francis said, scratching his head and refilling his mug with tea from the pot. "He doesn't seem the type."

"We have to let the guards know but in a way that's not traceable back to us. We've been trying to think of a way all the way from Mrs Stanley's house to here but we're coming up short. Any ideas? We were thinking maybe sign up to a VPN and a throwaway email account."

Francis McCabe threw his head back and howled with laughter. "Are you serious? The pair of ace detectives and you're asking me how you get that information across?"

"Yeah. It was a simple question," Fiona said, getting offended. "We know we're not good at this, but we're doing all we can."

"Ah, what am I supposed to do? You come in here with your suggestions about using anonymizers and the like."

"That's the reality of life these days, Dad. If we sent it from one of our phones they'd be able to trace it."

Francis rolled his eyes. "Who said anything about sending it from your phone? Come on, do you have any idea what you're dealing with here? Do you really think they're going to try and trace whatever message you send them?"

"They might."

"I doubt it. Anyway," he said, leaning back in his chair and staring up at the ceiling. "I have a better idea. I'll go down to Phelan's and tell Conway myself."

"You'll do *what*?"

"You heard me."

"That's like the opposite of what we've been talking about. What's the opposite of anonymous? Because that's exactly what you're suggesting."

"Nonsense," he said, waving his hand. "Think

about it. This is Conway we're talking about. I'll go down there and have a word in his ear. His memory'll be so fuzzy tomorrow he won't have a clue who told him what. He'll make up some story about an anonymous tip-off purely because he won't want to admit to the sarge that he was three sheets to the wind."

Fiona glanced at Marty and they both smiled. For once she was glad of Sergeant Brennan's rigid ways. The old sergeant was just as bad as Garda Conway and wouldn't have cared less that Conway was drunk when he got the tipoff.

10

"IT'LL WORK," Francis said the following morning. Usually at this time he'd have moved through to the international section, but he was still staring at the front page. It was obvious that he was beginning to doubt Garda Conway's memory of what he'd said the night before.

"It will," Marty agreed. He had stayed the night after they stayed up into the wee hours sitting around the table and discussing what could possibly have turned Alan Power into a cold-blooded killer.

They had concluded that it was the same thing that had swayed many people: greed.

"It had better work," Fiona said, pushing her dry toast around her plate. "But if it doesn't, we'll fall back on plan B. We'll find a way to send them an anonymous tip online."

Marty nodded. "And we better do it quick. The clock is ticking. We need to act before Power disappears with that money."

"What time is it?" Fi said, standing so abruptly the blood rushed to her head. "I didn't realise it was that late. My phone died last night and I don't have my charger. I'd better get to the pub."

"Sure there's no point. It's well past half eight. Any commuters looking for a coffee will be well gone by now. And you don't have a bit of food to offer them."

"What are you?" she asked laughing. "My anti-business adviser? I can't just stay closed for days on end."

"It's sort of an extreme situation. People will understand."

"You're right," she muttered, sitting back down. "Everybody probably knows at this stage. I bet I'd have done a roaring trade today with everybody skulking in trying to get the latest gossip out of me."

"Open up at lunch. Offer them meal specials and the chance to have their photo taken with the murderess's daughter."

Their father groaned and lowered his paper from his face. "Would ye not joke about it at the table? It's a bit too soon to see the funny side. For all we know, they'll ignore what I told them about Power and insist on keeping her in there and—"

The sound of a key in the front door made them all freeze and jerk their heads towards it.

"Who's that?"

"Don't know."

"Ben's upstairs."

"Kate probably," Fi said, disappointed.

"Ah." Francis hit his paper in disgust. "Where was she anyway, your sister? What was she doing out 'til all hours with her mother in the Garda station being questioned?"

The front door opened after much scraping. None of them paid much heed to it, assuming it was just Kate coming in after a big night out. A moment later, they realised their mistake.

"Look at the state of this hallway," said a loud voice from the other side of the door. "Would none of ye have thought of Hoovering, no? Is that too much to ask?"

They were on their feet in an instant. Marty gained an immediate head-start, his sporting prowess giving him a speed advantage. Fi was next, trailed by their father who had a gammy hip when it suited him and when there was an 'R' in the month.

"Mam," Marty cried, rushing through the door

71

and pulling Mrs McCabe into a bear hug despite her laughing protestations.

"Oh, Martin," she whispered, finally acknowledging that no amount of scolding was going to make him put her down. "Oh, it's so good to be home."

"They let you out."

"They did, Francis. Mammy had just come in to visit so I didn't think there was any sense in ringing you when she could just give me a lift."

"You're right, too. Ah, it's good to have you back, Margaret. What happened?" He cast a subtle glance in Fiona's direction as he said this.

Mrs McCabe dropped her handbag and bustled to the kitchen.

"I don't know," she said, after she'd filled the kettle with water and popped it on. "They came in this morning and said there'd been a development in the case. That I was free to go but I wasn't to travel out of the country without telling them first."

"Do they have anyone else in for it?"

"Not that I know of. Did you see anyone, Mammy?"

Granny Coyle shook her head, her mouth set in a grim line. "I did not, indeed." She reached over and took one of the dry slices of toast from the plate Fiona had abandoned. She held it up and twisted it in the air inches from her face, as if it was some ancient cypher she was struggling to translate. "What is this?"

"It's bread, Rose," Francis said, in a voice that suggested he'd had all he could take of his mother-in-law for a while.

"It doesn't look like bread to me. It looks hard and nasty. Like it came out of a packet three days ago."

"Well it was all that was left in the press."

"Francis McCabe! You're how old and you still have no idea how to look after yourself?"

"I'll make a fresh loaf," Mrs McCabe called.

"You will not, love. Will you sit down? You go and have a nice shower and I'll make it. Have you brown flour?"

"Of course. It's all in the press behind you."

Fiona closed her eyes and drowned out their words, listening instead to the melody of their voices.

"What're you looking so happy about?" her father barked.

Her eyes flew open and she shook her head. "It's over. Mam's home. Job done. I don't know what *you're* looking so *grumpy* about."

"I thought it was obvious."

She shook her head, searching his face for some

73

clue and growing impatient when he wouldn't elaborate. "No. Please explain."

He closed his paper and folded it in his prompt, precise way, obviously having concluded that he wasn't going to get a moment's peace for the rest of the day.

"Do you really think our job is done? I mean, sure, your mother is out. For the moment."

"What are you talking about, Dad? They know about Power."

"Ah, lookit, it could be nothing. I'm just saying don't relax too much. You heard what they told her about sticking around. I'm not going to let myself forget about this until I hear it on the news that they've got their man."

"Or woman," his wife piped up from the kitchen, where she was arguing over ingredients with her mother.

"Ah here, don't say that. It's fine here in the house, but if you say something like that in public they're only going to change their minds again and decide you're a suspect after all."

Mrs McCabe laughed. "I didn't say it was me. I was just saying. It was probably a woman."

Marty looked at Fi who looked at her father, who threw his hands up in the air.

"What on earth gave you that impression?"

"There's no need to take that tone with me, Francis," his wife said, coming out of the kitchen with her hands on her hips, like she did when she was well and truly riled up by something. "I'm only saying what I've heard from a number of different places through the years. It's women, isn't it Mammy?"

"I haven't the faintest idea what you're talking about, love," Margaret said without turning around. It was clear from the clouds of flour that she was wrestling her dough into submission.

"With the poison, I mean."

Francis baulked. "Who said anything about poison?"

"Brennan did," she said, still standing there in full confrontation mode. "That's how she was killed. It was poison."

"I thought they said she was murdered."

She shrugged. "She was. She was poisoned. They found traces of it in her system and they found the same stuff in the fry she'd been eating when she died. Imagine! The poor woman. Killed by her lovely breakfast."

"I thought you hated her," Fiona frowned. "After you caught her with your picture."

"Ah, sure it doesn't matter now. Maybe she got confused, the poor old thing. They do at that age. I wonder who did it? I can't think of anyone who disliked her that much."

"Power," Francis announced, stopping abruptly. It was obvious that he'd been about to tell her how he came by that information but thought better of it. *Wisely*, Fi thought.

"What? Where'd you hear that?"

He shrugged. "Garda Conway had a few too many down in Phelan's last night. It was he who told me."

Mrs McCabe frowned and shook her head, seemingly perplexed. "Is that so, now? Well I'm surprised by that. I've heard it said so many times."

"What?" Granny Coyle scoffed. "You're making no sense."

"Poisoners," Mrs McCabe said as if she could barely stay patient for a moment longer. "Are usually women."

At this, Granny Coyle's eyes lit up. "You're right! She's right! I heard the same thing said manys a time on the True Crime channel."

Fiona looked around. All of the others seemed amused, but she couldn't shake the feeling that there was something in her mother's theory. She had heard the same thing, hadn't she? And now that her mother mentioned it. But it was crazy, wasn't it? They'd caught Alan Power red-handed.

"Can you think of another woman in Ballycashel with a grudge against Mrs Stanley?"

Her mother nodded absently, clearly thinking it over. "No," she said after a while. "I can't think of anyone. I thought she was a right aul sourpuss, but she's never actually done anything to me. I can't remember hearing anyone giving out about her apart from Mammy."

They all turned to look at Granny Coyle.

"What?" she protested.

"You were giving out about Mrs Stanley?"

Rose nodded, suddenly cagy. "I suppose. She's a miserable aul one. Everyone knows that."

Fiona glanced at Marty, who looked very serious.

11
_____

FIONA RETURNED to the pub just before all hell broke loose between her mother and grandmother. She smirked as she unlocked the front door of the pub. It hadn't taken them even an hour to get back into their usual ways after Mrs McCabe's return from the Garda station. She didn't know why she'd expected anything else.

And it wasn't even about the case at all, but about which of them was going to make the bread.

"I like soda bread but they take it to extremes," she muttered, as she walked into the pub.

Her parents had run McCabes when she was growing up, but it was finally beginning to feel like her own place. She had painted the green walls a charcoal colour after experimenting with white and finding it far too light for a traditional Irish pub— even one that was trying to reinvent itself as a cocktail bar slash coffee shop. She shook her head. She hadn't been doing so well on the coffee shop front: she'd been opening up early in the mornings and serving espresso coffees and baked goods. The problem was there wasn't a whole lot of demand for that in Ballycashel. What commuters there were seemed more concerned about getting in their cars and getting up the motorway to Dublin or down to Cork as quickly as possible. It wasn't that the locals were opposed to a cafe, it was more that they were set in their ways. There was already a cafe—Mary's— which had been on the go for at least thirty years. It was where Fiona and her siblings had gone to buy their sausage rolls when their parents gave them money on a Friday to go and buy a treat for lunch.

Fi shook her head. There should have been plenty of room in town for two cafes, but she had underestimated people's unwillingness to try new things. Sure even people who had moved to the town when she was in primary school were still referred to as newcomers.

"I don't know," she muttered, grabbing her spray of surface cleaner and a fresh cloth from the press under the sink in the kitchen. "Maybe I should just stop opening early. I'd get a whole lot more sleep if I did, that's for sure."

She set about scrubbing down all of the tables and the bar counter. When she was finished, she looked around and decided the floors could use a good thorough clean.

When she was finished with that, her enthusiasm started to falter. The place was spotless and there was nothing left for her to do except to polish for the sake of it.

The problem was, it was far too early to open the bar—she'd just be sitting behind the counter, twiddling her thumbs. Nor did she want to go upstairs. She'd only end up watching TV and that was hardly productive, was it?

She shuffled behind the bar and hit the button that was concealed underneath on the staff side.

Within five minutes, the bell rang out above the door and her brother Marty appeared in the bar, hands full of little boxes.

"What have you got there?"

He held them up as if he was surprised to see them too. "Rat poison."

She shivered. "What on earth are you doing with that?"

"I was restocking the shelf when you buzzed. Thought there might be something wrong."

"Nah," she said, resting her chin on her hand and leaning on the bar. "I said I'd see what you were up to. I take it you got fed up with listening to them too."

He nodded. "Yeah. Listen, Fi, I'm a bit busy over in the shop. I'll catch you later, yeah?"

She watched him leave and decided to lock up after him just in case. Just in case what, she didn't know. They must have taken Power into custody by now—it was almost eleven.

She turned on the speaker system and selected a playlist of relaxing songs she liked. She'd never usually play it in the bar, but it was closed.

Try as she might, though, she couldn't stop her mind from returning to the murder. Why would Alan Power do away with Mrs Stanley? She had always seemed perfectly pleasant to Fiona. But her mother and granny felt differently. Mrs McCabe bugged the heads off her kids on a lot of occasions, but she wasn't exactly a difficult person. Even so, she had been riled up enough at Mrs Stanley that they'd had a screaming match in the street.

Before she knew what she was doing, Fiona found herself switching the music off and walking through the bar to the door. After locking up, she turned and walked as fast as she could, not stopping until she reached the Garda station.

This isn't exactly a good idea, she reflected, though that didn't stop her from hurrying up the steps.

She had taken to describing Ballycashel's Garda Sergeant as her arch nemesis and she wasn't joking. They couldn't stand the sight of each other. She didn't really understand why—they had gone on one terrible date in Dublin long before he ever got posted to Ballycashel. She hadn't called him back and he'd held a grudge against her ever since.

Even though he's a grown man in his thirties, she thought, getting riled up as she pushed open the door to the station.

Behind the desk, Garda Conway looked slightly the worst for wear. His cheeks were flushed a deep rosy colour and the bags under his eyes were even darker than usual.

"Morning Garda Conway," she called.

"Howaya Fiona. What can we do for you?"

She looked around, glad to see the sergeant's office door closed.

"Ah not much. I just wanted to come down and say... well, thanks for being so good to my mam when she was here."

It was a lie, but that wasn't important to her. All she wanted to do was hear that they'd thrown the book at Power and the case was closed. Of course, she couldn't come right out and just ask—Conway didn't give anything away when he was sober.

"Ah, not at all. It was a terrible business. We had to bring her in for questioning after she was seen fighting with poor Mrs Stanley."

"I know, I know. I appreciate you being so good to her." She paused and looked around. "How's your mother?"

"Ah, she's grand now. Can't complain. The arthritis is at her."

"And she must be rattled after what happened to poor old Mrs Stanley."

His eyes widened and for a moment she thought she'd pushed it too far, but then she saw there was no suspicion in them. For an officer of the peace, Garda Conway was an incredibly trusting soul. Part of her wanted to shake him and tell him to cop on; she was only trying to butter him up so that he'd give her information.

She was so conflicted that she didn't notice a door opening at the edge of her peripheral vision.

"Miss McCabe," said a cold voice.

Fiona stifled a groan. "Sergeant Brennan. What a pleasure."

"I'm surprised to see you back here so soon. What can we do for you?"

There was no sense in beating around the bush, she knew. Brennan may have been a pain, but at least he fit the model for an officer of the law. He was sharp and suspicious of everyone. There'd be no asking after his mother and hoping he'd spill the beans on the case. She couldn't even imagine what his mother might look like—she pictured a pointy-faced old biddy in a cashmere twinset living in a vast country pile in South County Dublin.

"I just popped in. I was wondering if there had been any developments in the case."

His features twisted in distaste. "Were you indeed?"

She nodded, though her heart sank as she realised that not only was he not going to tell her anything, but he was going to take immense pleasure in refusing to do so.

"You should know by now that I'm not able to comment on a live case."

"But it's solved. You've got your man." She bristled—she hadn't wanted to raise her voice or show her hand.

His smile widened as if he was getting great enjoyment out of this. "Is that so?"

She shrugged. "I don't know. I heard… I heard there was a break-in over at Mrs Stanley's house last night."

"Dear me," Sergeant Brennan said, glancing around. "You seem to know a lot about our case. Care to elaborate on your source?"

"Not at all," she said, breezily as she could. "It's just that a few people around here have mentioned that there was a man arrested."

"Have they now?"

She nodded. "That's what I just said."

He looked from her to Garda Conway and back, eyes narrowed suspiciously. "You're aware, Garda Conway, that you have a duty not to discuss Garda business with members of the public?"

Fiona gasped in outrage. "No, you have the wrong end of the stick there. It wasn't him who told me. It was... it was Mrs Roche. She said it to my granny after mass."

The sergeant made no response. He walked away, shaking his head, leaving Fiona looking apologetically at Conway.

"I'm sorry. I didn't mean to get you into trouble."

The old guard shrugged after throwing an extremely disparaging look in the direction of the sergeant's office. "Don't mind him. I know I didn't say anything and he can't prove a thing."

"Even still..."

"I'm telling you," Conway said almost cheerily. "Don't worry about it." He leaned a little closer and smiled conspiratorially. "And if he's going to accuse me of blabbing, then I might as well tell you this. We brought a fella in for questioning in relation to the matter, but he has a solid alibi for the time of the murder so he's been released without charge."

1 2

Far from feeling the matter was all wrapped up, Fiona was even more perplexed than ever when she finally got back to the pub. After half an hour, she realised there was no way she was going to relax until she was busy with customers. With a sigh, she hurried upstairs and changed into her running clothes.

Running always helped her to calm down and clear her head—even if she didn't particularly enjoy the activity. Her natural instinct was to stop running and walk after she began to feel breathless but she forced herself to keep on going, reminding herself of the time she'd actually managed to run that ten kilometre charity race in town a few years back.

After ten minutes, she hit a nice stride, though she obviously hadn't succeeded in fully clearing her head. She realised with a start that she'd taken a different route to normal. Now she was directly in the path of Mrs Stanley's house. There were no other roads off this one until she passed the house—it was either keep going or turn around.

"It's fine," she muttered to herself.

Even though it wasn't. Her pulse climbed even higher than it had when she'd sprinted to the lights to cross Main Street. There was nobody around and anyone who lived nearby was likely to be at work.

Normally that wouldn't bother her—after all, it was part and parcel of small town life. Today it did. She couldn't stop thinking about how they'd had such a narrow escape from Alan Power. If he'd come any earlier, they might not have heard him. He would have walked straight in on them and they might not have made it out of there...

Fiona's train of thought vanished as she ran past the old Miller house, where they had hidden the night before. Nobody had lived in it since she'd been old enough to wander around the town and she didn't ever remember meeting the mysterious Millers. Now, though, there was every indication that it wasn't abandoned.

There was a moving van parked in the driveway,

just a few feet from where they had lurked the night before. She stopped and stared, horrified. Had the van been there the night before? She couldn't think. She'd seen the outline of a large tree, but hadn't paid attention to anything else. Besides, it was parked so close to the house that it was unlikely it would have stood out to them.

"Oh my God," she muttered, staring aghast. Had there been somebody there watching them as they watched Alan?

"Hi there!"

Fiona started and looked up, surprised to see a young man about her age standing in the porch. She was even more amazed when she realised she knew him.

"Angus!" she said, hurrying through the open gate. "What are you doing here? I didn't realise you worked for a moving company."

He looked up and she couldn't help but see the way his face lit up on seeing her—or had she just imagined it?

"I don't."

She shook her head, glancing at the van uncertainly. Yes, there was no doubt about it—it was a moving van alright. It said so right across the side in neon orange lettering.

"Ah," he laughed, following her gaze. "I don't

work for a moving company. I just hired the van. Did Colm not tell you?"

Angus was a friend of her brother's from college. He had helped Fiona with a little problem she'd had a few months before by pretending to be her German boyfriend. Fiona had been surprised to find herself getting more into the charade than she had expected: Angus had a twinkle in his eye and a dimple in his left cheek that she'd found herself thinking about again and again in the months since.

"No," she said, shaking her head. "That's brothers for you. I thought you were moving to Edinburgh."

He laughed. "I did. After a few months I realised that transferring with the same company was a big mistake. So I handed in my notice and left. I had a great time here before that so I thought I'd look for a place to rent while I consider my next move. Maybe you can give me some tips on packing up my life and starting afresh."

It was her turn to laugh. "I can't say I'm an expert. Actually, if anything I've been neglecting the pub because of all the action that's been happening around here."

"Action?"

She shook her head and waved it away as if it was nothing. She'd just been struck by the strangest urge to play down the severity of the murder case. She didn't know why: maybe it was on the off chance that he might change his mind and jump back in the van and hightail it back to Scotland.

"It's nothing. So you're moving to Ballycashel?"

He nodded. "Yeah, that's the plan anyway. Found this place. They were only too happy to rent it out to me and it's not in too bad condition. Apparently, the owners come over every month or so to air out the inside, though the garden will need a lot of work." He paused and stared into her eyes. "Colm never mentioned anything about me moving here?"

"No," she said, shaking her head. "But does that surprise you? That lad'd forget his head if it wasn't screwed onto his body."

"He would and all. Still, I'm surprised he didn't mention it."

"Ah, that's Colm," Fiona said, thinking no more about it. "Anyway, I'd better keep moving if I'm to get back to the pub in time to open later. Welcome to the area! We'll have to throw you a welcome party in the pub when…" She stopped. She'd been about to say 'when things calm down around here'. She smiled. "When you're all settled in."

His face lit up. "I'd like that, Fiona. That sounds great."

She turned and began to jog up the road, all thoughts of the murder case pretty much forgotten now.

13

———————————————————

IT WAS a slow evening at the pub. Fiona would have been disgusted by that if she hadn't bumped into Angus that afternoon. Now that she had, she was glad of the quiet time. It had been a long time since she'd sat around daydreaming about a man—not that she'd ever admit to anyone that that was what she was doing.

As time passed, people began to trickle in. Soon there were a handful of people dotted around the bar. She smiled as she changed playlists on the sound system, telling herself she needed something she could dance to behind the bar in order to stop herself from sitting there like a soppy teenager.

It did the trick immediately. She closed her eyes and swayed around behind the bar. She knew every inch of it—not just from running it herself, but from playing behind there as a child. She had kept the original bar, unable to even contemplate getting rid of it.

She was so engrossed in the music that she didn't hear the bell ring to let her know somebody else had entered the bar. Or, rather, the music was too loud for her to hear it. The first indication she had that something had changed was the strange chill that ran through her.

Its cause became clear a few seconds later.

"What's that racket?"

Fiona's heart sank. Mrs Davis stood in front of her, her green eyes burning with anger. "Music." Mrs Davis had never been more than barely civil to her, but this was the first time they'd ever really spoken face-to-face. The woman owned the building behind the pub and the hardware shop, and she liked things just so. Her little clothes shop appeared to still be open, even though it had had the same window display for what felt like years.

"Doesn't sound like music to me."

Fiona shook her head. "I'm sorry Mrs Davis, but it's no louder than we've played it on other nights. Even when Dad ran this place, they had trad bands in all the time that were far louder than this."

Mrs Davis pursed her lips. A young couple

walked into the bar behind her and Fiona nodded at them, signalling that she'd be with them in a moment.

"I don't care what you used to do. I'm telling you it's too loud."

Fiona shook her head. It was loud, but not excessively so. When she had taken over the pub and installed a new sound system, they had gone to the trouble of measuring the decibel level that could be heard outside and in the hardware shop. Fiona was well aware of how loud each volume level on the system would sound not just in the pub but outside as well.

"I've just got a new hearing aid," Mrs Davis added, just as Fiona was reaching for the remote to turn the volume down. "And now I can't hear myself think."

Fiona quietened the music a bit and smiled. "Maybe it'll take a while to get used to the new sharpness in your hearing." She knew all about how it took a bit of getting used to: Granny McCabe had driven them all mad when she got her first hearing aids in. She'd been unable to do anything in public for weeks while she got used to the sharpness.

Mrs Davis, however, did not take Fiona's remark in the spirit in which it was intended. She narrowed her eyes as if she'd just been mortally offended. "I'll thank you to turn the volume down now, young lady. Or I'll be forced to call the Gardaí."

"It is down," Fiona murmured, shaking her head in disbelief. But there was no point in her even saying it: she was speaking to Mrs Davis's stiff departing back.

"Isn't she a dear?" Louise Graham remarked to the man who had accompanied her into the bar a few moments before.

Fiona had seen them around town together several times and assumed they were going out. She couldn't for the life of her think of his name so she took their drinks order and then busied herself rearranging the crisps behind the bar once she'd given them their drinks.

It was definitely a shortcoming for a bar owner, she concluded, to have such a terrible memory for names. She had resorted to tricks like repeating a person's name in her head as she was introduced to them, but nothing she tried ever seemed to work.

She focussed on tidying, her attention drifting in and out of their conversation. From the sounds of it, Louise was talking about her weight-lifting. She had tried to convince Fiona to join the little gym she trained at, but Fi had politely declined, fearing injury.

"It was awful," Louise was saying. "Kev was

supposed to be spotting me when I was going for a squat PB. I don't know what he was at. I ended up losing my balance and he wasn't there to help with the bar. Now it feels like I've really strained my trapezius. I mean, this might rule me out of the nationals. He talks as if he's really interested in the club, but he's not pulling his weight."

"That's terrible," her companion said, shaking his head. "But you were lucky it wasn't more serious. I'll have a word with him if you want."

Fiona couldn't help but wince. From the way Louise was sitting, it looked like she was in a good deal of pain, and the man with her didn't consider that a serious injury? She hated to imagine what he might view as serious. Regardless, she was glad she'd declined Louise's offer and decided to stick to running and working with lighter weights.

"No," Louise said, waving her hand. "I suppose the timing isn't so bad what with me starting primary teaching in a few weeks."

"Even still. It's not on. What about the others who train there?"

A short while later, the door opened again. Fiona smiled at the sight of Mrs Roche, a good friend of her granny's.

"Brandy for you, Mrs Roche?"

The old woman nodded. "Thanks, love." Her face

grew serious. "Terrible business about your poor mother."

Fi winced. Granny Coyle had sworn she wouldn't mention a word about it to anyone. So how did Agnes Roche know about it?

Mrs Roche eyed her cagily. "No offence. It's all around town. I thought you'd know that—a small place like Ballycashel."

Fiona sighed and reached for a glass, pausing before she turned to the bottles. "Will Mrs Finnegan be joining you today?"

"She will, she will. Better make it two."

Things got busy then and Fiona forgot all about the spectre hanging over her family. She chatted and served drinks, completely in her element. It was only when customers began to filter away that her thoughts returned to the problem at hand.

Round and round the details of the case went in her head. It was odd in the extreme, even more so since they had all but caught Power red-handed. But hadn't he been released?

It was still only early. By rights, she should have kept the pub open until ten or eleven if she had any hope of making a proper go of it, but it was a quiet night.

After another thirty minutes of boredom, she gave up and grabbed her jacket. She wouldn't rest until she figured out what was going on, she knew. For a fleeting minute, she considered going to the Garda station and trying to butter up the sergeant, but she soon saw that plan for the desperate, deluded idea that it was.

She decided instead that she'd go back to her parents' house and see how everyone was coping. Secretly she hoped that the whole thing would have resolved itself; that the guards would realise they'd been handed the real murderer on a plate.

14

THAT WASN'T THE CASE, as she found out when she got back. She tried to pretend she was fine as she ate, but not even ten minutes after sitting on the couch in the sitting room, she could hold it in no longer.

"It's driving me mad."

Marty glanced at her before returning his gaze to the telly. "What, this? I'd say it was boring more than anything."

Fiona looked at the television. It had been on ever since she'd arrived at her parents' house, but she'd been so worked up she hadn't even noticed what was on it. She shook her head.

"I'm not talking about Ireland's Next Best Singer, you eejit," she hissed, careful not to arouse their parents' suspicions. "I'm talking about the case. Mrs Stanley's murder. Isn't it driving you mad?"

"Hush, you two," Mrs McCabe called from the other sofa. "They're about to announce who won this week's immunity challenge."

Fiona rolled her eyes, impatient to get out of there. It hadn't been a good idea to call over, she realised. She needed something to take her mind off things, not time to stew over her problems. She should have gone for another run, she thought.

"Yeah, I suppose," Marty said finally. "It might explain why I put the vegetable seeds where the slug pellets should go earlier on. It's weird, like. Someone obviously had it in for Mrs Stanley, but who? I know granny said she was sour, but she's an old lady. Couldn't hurt a fly. And Alan Power. What exactly was he doing over there? They're not related, and I've never heard of him being involved with the elderly community. Come to think of it, I've never heard of him being involved with much of anything —he keeps himself to himself. And now he's breaking into an old woman's house?"

"A murdered old woman's house," Fiona said with a shiver. "I know, right. It's—"

Their father let out an exaggerated sigh. "Ah here, for the love of God. If you're going to natter all the way through it, you might as well go out to the kitchen and let the rest of us watch it in peace."

"He has a point. Come on," Fiona said, standing and hurrying past the TV as quickly as she could. "We'll chat out here."

"About time," Francis McCabe groaned.

———

"OH HEY, GRANNY," Fiona said, going out to the kitchen. "Why are you sitting out here and not in there with the rest of them?"

Rose Coyle sighed. "I can't stand that singing programme. That's what they're watching, isn't it? I could hear the stupid screams of them as I came up the path."

"It sure is. I'm not a big fan of it either."

"What were you watching it for then? What else would they have on at this time?"

"Ah, yeah." She filled the kettle with water from the tap and shook her head. "Normally I'd take refuge in the flat when they're watching it, but I couldn't settle today. This case. Is it not driving you mad?"

"Not so much now that my daughter's been cleared of any wrongdoing."

"Has she, though? I thought they released her on the understanding that she had to stick around."

There was definite annoyance in Granny Coyle's voice now. "They don't know what they're at, those guards. It's obvious it wasn't Margaret. She's all bark and no bite: a good sergeant would know that from living around her for as long as he has. It's not like Ballycashel is a big place."

"No," Fiona said, dropping three cups to the table and returning for the milk. They were sitting at the smaller table in the kitchen, not the dining table they used for meals. Fiona preferred this one—it was cosier and there was something so homely and reassuring about the oilskin tablecloth with the cupcake pattern on it. It was probably older than Fiona herself.

"If you ask me, he should pay more heed to the people around here; the ones whose taxes pay his wages."

"You won't get any argument from us on that front," Marty nodded, retrieving the biscuit tin from the sideboard.

"I hear ye did a bit of investigating," Granny Coyle said, helping herself to a biscuit.

Fiona glanced at her older brother and shook her head. It wasn't a gesture of surprise—more of resignation. She was beyond marvelling at their grandmother's ability to know everything that was going on in the town, often before anyone else.

"Granny, you should be the sergeant around here. You certainly have your ear to the ground."

She looked affronted. "Sure didn't I work in the civil service for years? And you'd have me go out there again? Have I not earned the right to relax and enjoy the finer things in life, like a good creamy Guinness and the occasional trip to the pictures?"

"And an annual gallivant off to Lourdes."

If Granny had appeared affronted before, she looked positively disgusted now. "How could you say such a thing? I'll have you know that we were there on pilgrimage."

Fiona rearranged her features into something resembling a straight face, but Marty couldn't be saved. "Sure you were," he said with a smirk.

Granny Coyle slammed the lid on the biscuit tin and pushed it away from her. It was a telling move for a woman with a sweet tooth as well-developed as hers. "First my daughter gets arrested. Then my own grandchildren spread salacious stories about me." She sighed and shook her head.

"Ah come off it Granny," Fiona said, opening the biscuit box again. "Mam gives us the hard-done-by treatment enough without you starting the same thing."

There was a painful pause, during which Fi wondered if she'd gone too far. Then her grandmother's features lightened and she grinned. "It was a hell of a time over in Lourdes. You should have seen the look on your brother's face when he cottoned on to the fact that we weren't just a bunch of aul fuddy duddies wanting to take baths in holy water."

"I can imagine. He was still pretty shell-shocked when he told us."

Fiona went to retrieve the teapot from the cooker. She placed it onto one of the cork tablemats with such force that it silenced the others and seemed to punctuate the conversation. She looked from one to the other, realising the significance of it and deciding to go with it.

"This thing's been driving me mad, Granny. Marty's the same. Who could have killed Mrs Stanley, do you think? I'm sure you know—we saw who broke into her house last night. It was Alan Power, but he's been released without charge. He has an alibi apparently."

They both watched Granny Coyle, as if they hoped she'd be the one who held the key to making sense of it all. Disappointment shot through Fi when the older woman pursed her lips a few minutes later and shook her head.

"I don't know why you're looking to me for answers. I don't know the man at all."

Fiona sighed and reached for the teapot, pouring them all a generous cup. "Nothing at all? You know everyone in town."

"Everyone in town of a certain age, my love. He's a recent enough transplant and he's got no time for an old biddy like me."

"You're not an old biddy."

"Well I know that and you know that, but we have to be realistic about these things. Anyway, it's not just me. He's never really had much time for anyone and he's not well liked around the place at all."

"What does he do?"

Granny Coyle shrugged. "Some computer business or other? I'm not sure. All I know is he commutes to Dublin every day and he doesn't have time for anyone around here. Maureen Delaney's son lives up there. I think he works for the same company."

Fiona shook her head. Why would an IT professional be breaking into old women's houses in the dark and then denying it when the guards came knocking on his door? "I wonder what his alibi was."

Their grandmother took a huge swig of tea. "I expect he was at work at the time the poison was administered. They would have worked it back by now and figured out a time window for when it happened. It's remarkable how much they can narrow these things down nowadays."

They both stared at her open-mouthed. Marty was the first to be able to verbalise his astonishment. "How the hell do you know that? Have you been chatting up Garda Conway?"

"Marty! How can you say such a thing! She's our grandmother."

Granny Coyle threw her head back and laughed. "Ah, you don't have to be affronted on my behalf, dearie. You know, it's not far from the truth. Maybe I'll have to go making fluttery eyes at Garda Conway, as Martin says. No, it's amazing how much you'd pick up from watching the True Crime channel. Honest to God, it's gruesome stuff at times but it's fascinating."

Fiona allowed this to sink in. Finally, she looked from her brother to their grandmother and back, a plan forming. "What do you both say to trying to solve this thing ourselves," she said at last. "We've got nothing to lose."

"I'm in," Granny Coyle said without hesitation. "On one condition."

"What's that?"

"That you don't leave me out of any of the fun. If

you're going on a stakeout, I want to be informed. Got it?"

"Ah, but Granny, it was stupid of us. We could have got in serious trouble..."

"Is that a 'no', Martin?" Her voice was pure ice.

"Not at all, Granny. I just don't want to get you in trouble—or worse."

On hearing that, she became even more scornful. "Haven't I been getting into trouble—or worse—since long before either of ye were even thought of? Never mind ye, since before your parents came on the scene! And you try to shelter me from trouble?"

"Never mind," Marty muttered, no doubt wondering why he'd bothered. "Okay, I promise."

"I promise too," Fiona said with a grin. "Okay, so what do we know? I'll go get a pen and paper. Marty, you make more tea. We're going to need it."

15

As soon as she opened her eyes the next morning, Fiona rolled over and picked up the crumpled notepad from the bedside table. She blinked as she looked at her caffeine-induced scribbles from the night before.

In the cold light of day, their 'findings', as they'd dubbed them, seemed a lot less significant than they had the night before.

Granny didn't know much about Alan Power, but she had had quite a bit to say about Mrs Stanley. Fiona had diligently written it all down, excited about the possibility of discovering something new. Now, with an objective eye, she saw there wasn't much to go on. Certainly, there was nothing on the list that explained why the old woman had been murdered.

She sat up and stared at her messy handwriting.

Granny Coyle had known Mrs Stanley since they were both newly-married young women. And she had always been wary of the woman.

Fiona had seized on this and waited, pen hovering to capture the details that would help them solve the case.

As it turned out, Granny Coyle had nothing concrete on her. It was more of a gut feeling. In fairness, Fiona had learned that her grandmother's gut instincts were usually to be trusted, but she still couldn't help feeling a little disappointed by the lack of hard evidence.

The list was hardly ground-breaking—it took up just one A4 page of lined notepaper, but when you looked more closely at it, that was more due to Fiona's messy handwriting than anything. The core of it boiled down to this.

1. Mrs Stanley is shifty. Wouldn't look at you in the shop or at mass. Would only speak to you if she wanted something.

2. She had huge internet bills according to Niamh from the post office, where she paid her bills each

month. (Granny thinks it's online poker, but probably Skyping her sister in America?)

3. Always went to bingo on the first Saturday of every month.

4. Kept herself to herself.

5. Very particular. Mrs Finnegan did a bit of cleaning for her years ago when she had the money but the arrangement only lasted a week. Mrs Stanley complained that the place wasn't clean enough.

ON AND ON IT WENT. Several snippets of information, all useless.

Except, something was niggling at the back of Fiona's mind. Something on the list should have jumped out at her, she felt, but it wasn't doing so.

"What is it I'm not seeing?"

She threw off the duvet and jumped out of bed, feeling around on the floor with her feet for her slippers. It was still reasonably warm outside, but the polished floorboards were cold underfoot. She shook her head, telling herself not to get distracted by unimportant things.

She got downstairs and turned on the coffee machine, before wandering into the bar kitchen to see what she could eat. There was nothing upstairs, save for the remnants of a round of camembert and some broken crackers, and she didn't feel like that. What she really wanted, she thought suddenly, was a big proper breakfast. She looked around in the cupboards, certain she could piece it together but in a roundabout way. She had the black pudding for the salads; Turkish bread and the spicy mixed beans she used to garnish some of the dishes on the menu. And she had plenty of eggs as always. It wasn't perfect, but it would at least resemble a full Irish breakfast. It seemed like a waste to go to all that effort just for one person, but she was too tired to go all the way to her parents' house and besides, her mother was trying to cut down on saturated fats, so it was more likely to be porridge on the menu rather than bacon and eggs.

She froze. Wasn't that what they'd found at Mrs Stanley's house? They'd found traces of poison in the half-eaten fry on the table.

She returned the black pudding to the fridge and decided she'd settle for porridge. Her appetite was suddenly gone.

Fi sat at the bar nursing her coffee. After a few sips, it finally struck her. She had a dull memory of hearing her granny tell some story about Mrs Roche never missing the bingo.

Maybe she knows something about Mrs Stanley that we don't.

She pulled out her phone to call Rose.

"Yeah, Agnes is mad for the bingo."

"Can we chat to her? If she goes all the time and Mrs Stanley did too…?"

"Hold on a minute, love." There was a strange muffled sound, as if she had covered the phone with her hand and was talking to someone in the background. "Anyway, where was I? Oh, yes. I suppose I can say it to her."

Fiona frowned. Her granny was known for her nocturnal habits, and she was seldom seen out and about before midday, except on Sundays when she went to eleven o'clock mass and it wasn't even nine o'clock yet. "Where are you?"

Granny Coyle laughed. "None of your concern." That muffled sound again. Fiona thought she could hear a man's voice and she just about made out the word 'Conway'.

"Granny! Where are you? Is there a man there with you?"

"Ah, Fiona you're awful provincial. I'm disappointed to see that."

"I'm not at all," Fi protested. "I just want to know why I heard a man's voice when my grandmother lives alone and usually doesn't get up this early."

"Maybe I got myself a toyboy?"

Fiona cringed. She did not want to think about such things, not even if it gave her over-worked mind a break from thinking about the case. "Really? I'm sure I heard you speak to Garda Conway. He's hardly a toyboy."

"I have to go," Rose Coyle announced. "I've got work to do."

Fiona stared at her phone, uncomprehending. It was the first she'd heard of it, and hadn't Granny Coyle *just* chastised Marty the day before for having the cheek to suggest she go and get a job?

"I don't know," she muttered, at a loss now. "I suppose I should open the pub."

She'd been slack in recent days, especially since her mother's arrest. The funny thing was, though, staying closed in the mornings had barely impacted her takings. At least, that was her suspicion. She realised with a sinking feeling that it had been at least two weeks if not more since she had actually taken the time to sit down and look at her books. Everything was automated through online bookkeeping software, but what good was that when you didn't even look at the charts they provided?

She looked around, suddenly fiercely protective of her little bar and all the time she had put into making it her own.

With all thoughts of the case forgotten, she took her coffee and hurried upstairs to her laptop.

Fi was so deep into her spreadsheets and calculations that it took a while for her to notice the noise; a sound that appeared to be coming from right outside her window. Frowning, she closed her laptop and went to the window, pen still in hand from furiously scribbling notes.

The sound got louder as she moved. She realised with a start that there was somebody banging on the door of the pub.

Alarm shot through her. She'd had her phone with her the whole time—if it was somebody she knew, they would have just called her instead of banging loud enough to disturb the whole street.

"That's not knocking," she muttered. "It's disturbing the peace. I should call Robocop, see how he feels about it."

The thought crossed her mind that it was in some way related to the case; that it might be the real murderer coming to exact revenge, but she was so curious that she put all caution. Besides, she was all the way upstairs and hadn't Marty replaced the locks after the last murder in Ballycashel.

She shivered. The *last* murder. What was going on? It was supposed to be a sleepy little town in the middle of Ireland, not somewhere that murders happened.

She could not reflect on that disturbing thought for very long because someone was still banging on the door and it sounded like they were getting even more impatient. She feared it would give her a headache if she let it continue—or worse, that it might draw Mrs Davis out to complain. She reached up and unlocked the sash window, pulling it up enough to let her lean out. Whoever it was was blocked by the little canopy above the pub door.

"Who is it? Did it cross your mind that we're closed and there's nobody in there to open it for you?" she yelled, before she could stop herself.

What if it was a customer or a supplier? Fiona cringed. She still hadn't mastered the art of being pleasant, no matter how hard she tried. It just wasn't instinctive. She waited at the window, hoping to God it wasn't a pub critic from the Saturn or the Times, about to shatter her already-shaky dreams of self-employment.

A grey head appeared from under the awning. Fiona had to blink to make sure she wasn't dreaming.

"Granny, what on earth are you doing? I thought it was a grown man down there with the force of that banging."

Granny Coyle looked far from pleased. "Well sure

what was I supposed to do? You wouldn't open the door and you weren't at your mammy's so I knew well you must be here."

Fi rolled her eyes. "Oh come on. Does nobody think I have any kind of a life at all? There are loads of places I might have been."

Rose didn't respond to that, but her expression said it all.

"What is it? What has you banging on my door like a woman possessed?"

"Get down here and let me in and I'll tell you. And put on that kettle. I'm dying for a cup of tea. The tea at the station tastes like dishwater, I'm telling you."

"The station?" Fiona shook her head. "What station were you at? They don't even have a cafe at the train station, isn't that why I thought it was a great idea to start doing coffees in the morning?"

"A fat lot of good that did for you."

Fi cringed. "What do you mean by that?" She'd had her suspicions, which she'd just confirmed by taking a close look at her takings versus the hours she'd been open in the past two weeks. Opening in the morning hadn't made a blind bit of difference to her profit levels once she factored in her time, not even at half the minimum wage. She hadn't told anyone about that yet; nor did she intend to.

"Sure isn't it obvious. Anyway, this isn't the time or the place for it. I'll tell you once you come down here and let me in. What's it going to look like—an old woman on your doorstep, starving for a little drop of tea?"

Fi hurried downstairs to open the door before anyone overheard and accused her of elder abuse.

16

"ABOUT TIME."

"The door was locked, Granny. What do you expect me to do, leave it wide open when I'm upstairs? It's not the eighteen hundreds, or whatever century you were born in."

"Oh, you cheeky madam. And I after putting myself out to find out more about Mrs Stanley's murder for you." She breezed past Fi into the bar. "I've a good mind not to tell you what I found out."

"Chance'd be a fine thing," Fiona muttered under her breath.

"What was that?"

"Nothing."

"I heard you."

"Why'd you ask so?"

"To test you," Granny Coyle said ominously, planting herself on one of the stools at the bar. "Now, make me a cuppa and I might see fit to tell you what I found out down at the Garda station."

Fiona froze in her tracks. "The Garda station? I'm not surprised you were down there, but you're telling me you found something out about the case? What, was Robocop off getting his mechanical body serviced or something?"

"No, but he may have become indisposed all the same."

"How'd you mean? Isn't that a bit coincidental…" Fiona narrowed her eyes. "What did you do?"

"I'm insulted you'd even ask such a thing…"

Fiona didn't miss the twinkle in her grandmother's eye. "What did you do?" she asked again, holding the teacup between them as if she might not hand it over if Granny Coyle didn't answer.

Rose smiled and shook her head. "Did no-one ever tell you you shouldn't come between a woman and her tea? Ah, it was nothing. I suppose I thought I might get in there before Sergeant Brennan if I got in early, but he was there in his office, all prim and proper as usual. Well, I thought I'd bring him a nice coffee to start the day."

"You did what?"

"Oh, don't look at me like that, sweetheart. No, I thought I'd bring him a nice coffee, and wasn't it an awful shame that I happened to get out my eye drops at the same time. You wouldn't believe it—didn't my hand shake and half the bottle fell into his coffee."

The cup and saucer slipped from Fi's hand and smashed all over the counter. She jumped out of the way just in time to avoid the hot liquid.

"Watch out, love. That tea is hot," Rose said casually.

"Granny, I can't believe what I'm after hearing. You're telling me you went in there and poisoned... *poisoned* the sergeant. What possessed you? Do you know how much trouble—"

"Relax, love. You sound just like your mother. I saw it on the telly. It doesn't cause any harm, you know. It just makes you a little... agitated, I suppose you'd call it. I have to admit I was a bit sceptical as to whether it'd work, but sure enough, his eyes got very wide and he hurried away awful fast to the toilet. After telling me not to touch anything—the cheek of him."

"And did you?" Fi asked, not even bothering to clean up the tea that was now dripping onto the floor from the bar. "Did you touch anything?"

"Of course I did, love." And with that, Granny Coyle stood up, straightened herself out, and pulled a sheaf of a4 pages out from underneath her knitted jumper.

Fiona nearly fainted. "What's that?"

"The case file," Rose said, casual as anything. "I was as surprised as you are. You'd think in this day and age it'd be all electronic, what with everyone trying to save the planet. But no, they print it all out and keep it in folders down at the station."

"I wasn't surprised that it was a paper file," Fiona managed to say. "I was more wondering what on earth you were doing with it. He's going to come after you as soon as he knows it's missing."

"Oh, he won't do that."

"I don't know. If you were the last person he saw when he had the file, then I'm sure he'll put two and two together. He may be an idiot but he's got at least half a brain cell in there somewhere."

"He won't suspect a thing," Rose said, sounding no less upbeat. "I photocopied it see. He won't even know I touched it. I was out of that office as soon as I had it. By the time he came out of the jacks with a big frown on his face, I was out at the desk chatting to Garda Conway again."

"So that's where you were when I rang you. You were waiting for the sergeant to pop out."

"I was. You were accusing me of all sorts. Now you see why I couldn't really speak. Anyway, enough of that. I got the file—that's the important thing. Do you want to see it?"

Fi looked at her as if it was a trick question. "Of course I do. Why'd you even need to ask?"

Rose grinned. "Go and make me another cup of tea then, love. And try not to spill it all over yourself this time."

17

"You realise this is highly illegal?" Fiona said, with not much conviction at all.

The truth was, she was dying to see what was in those pages, but the seriousness of her grandmother's actions still did not escape her.

"I hadn't really thought about it, Fiona. But yes. Now that you mention it, I understand."

"Do you?" Fiona fiddled with the handle of her cup. She had brought them a pot of tea and a plate of biscuits on a tray and they were comfortably enclosed in the snug. She loved that spot. She had many happy childhood memories of having gang meetings in there with her brothers and sister when they were convinced they were the Secret Seven.

Even now, sitting in there gave her a great sense of comfort and calm.

"Lookit," Rose said, looking Fi straight in the eyes. "I know well what I've gotten myself into. But you take a look through those pages and you'll understand why I don't care about the law at this moment in time."

"What do you mean?"

"Take a look." Rose pointed to the pile of pages, before grabbing them up and flicking through them. "No, I'll show you. Hold on a minute."

Fiona watched as she licked her finger and flicked through the pages, occasionally stopping and skimming through the contents of a sheet before continuing her search. She did this for a few minutes, before she nodded and handed Fi a single sheet.

"There."

"What am I looking at?" It appeared to be some kind of report, with loads of boxes and borders and tiny text in long, hard-to-read paragraphs. Her eyes tore across it as she struggled to make sense of what she was supposed to be seeing.

"It's their report about the interview with Alan Power," Rose said, taking a sip of her tea. "Read it."

Fiona's eyes grew wide with astonishment as she started to read and realised that, yes, she was actually looking at the police report that she had spent so long wondering about. It became clear why they had been so quick to let Power go.

He'd been in Dublin on the day of the murder. Now, she felt sure that lots of people lied and said they were somewhere they weren't, especially if they'd been arrested for murder.

This was different.

It wasn't just a transcript of the interview with Power, it was a summary of the proceedings which was annotated with follow-up work the Gardaí had done to prove or disprove his story.

He'd been working in Dublin on the day of the murder and his company had provided access card records as well as CCTV footage to confirm it. He'd been there from the early morning right through to the afternoon when he left for a meeting.

Fiona's eyes widened. "He never went back to the office! Granny, look!"

Rose shook her head and returned her attention to the pile of pages. "They estimate time of death was one or before one. Power used his swipe card to exit the building at half past twelve. He was caught on CCTV leaving the building. Even if he drove that day instead of taking the train, there's still no way he'd have made it back to Ballycashel in time. The poison was fast but it still took some time to act."

Fiona sat back and absorbed this. "He might not

have been there, but what if he hired somebody to do the job for him? He waited until he was sure it was done so he had an alibi. Then he went to check they'd done it right."

Rose stroked her chin for a few moments before nodding to the sheet. "Keep reading. They checked his phone records."

Fiona skimmed over the tiny, typed words. "And found nothing," she finished. She sighed. "He's an IT expert. Maybe he had ways of communicating with the killer that are undetectable."

"She was poisoned, love. That suggests she knew the killer or else she wouldn't have eaten while they were there."

"What if they snuck in? There was no sign of a break-in but they could have used the spare key we found."

"I can't imagine there's many hired killers roaming the streets of Ballycashel."

Fi shivered. "I hope not. So what does all this mean?"

Rose finished her tea and refilled her cup from the pot. "It means we need to look elsewhere. It's obvious Alan Power isn't our poisoner."

"No," Fiona said thoughtfully. "But he's definitely the guy who broke into Mrs Stanley's house that night. I'm sure of it. Why would he do that?"

Rose shook her head. "Maybe he heard she had money. Lord knows I don't know who would have told him that. Everyone thought she was poor as a church mouse."

"He was carrying something when we saw him. This report doesn't even mention a search of his house. What did he take?" She flicked through the pages, looking for something that might help them figure it out. There was report after report, but she couldn't find what she was looking for. She sighed. "Was there a list of everything they found in Mrs Stanley's house?"

"No," Rose said. "No, I didn't come across anything like that. I suppose it was because it had already been burgled when they found her. They fingerprinted the place but didn't come up with anything."

Fiona rifled through the pages until she came to the list of evidence that had been photographed in place and then taken from the house.

"I didn't copy the photos," Rose said. "I was afraid they'd jam in the copier."

Fi nodded, barely paying attention as she looked through the list. When she was done she sighed—it didn't tell them anything. "They took all the dishes that were in the sink as well as all the knives and anything else that could have been used as a weapon.

That's it. We're none the wiser. Hold on." She flicked back to the page and skimmed the list. "Two tea cups, two plates, two forks, two knives and a teapot. It looks like she had company for that last meal. That means she definitely knew her killer.

"There was no sign of her being involved in a struggle. The killer must have ransacked the place after the poison took effect. There was no DNA found on the other dishes so they must have taken care to clean them. Unless they were left over on the draining board from Mrs Stanley's dinner the night before."

"No," Rose said immediately. "She was tidy. Obsessively so. If there were dishes out they wouldn't have been out for long. I'm telling you."

Fi shook her head. "So that rules out Alan Power. He didn't have time to get back to the train station, let alone to get here and sit down for a meal with Mrs Stanley."

"It doesn't seem that way. So what was he doing there?"

"I don't know. I don't get it. She had a huge flat-screen telly and a state-of-the-art computer. And she had tickets sitting in the sideboard for Fort Lauderdale. But her bank statements are all here and she had no income apart from the pension. There's no sign of any of these transactions. And there's no sign of any money from the wind turbine company."

"Are you sure? Give me a look."

Fi handed it over.

Rose shook her head. "I suppose it's not that surprising. I've heard that those companies are very eager to get you to sign their contracts but it can take months or even years to get the turbines in. We would have known all about it if they'd started installing them."

"Where did she get the money then? And why did someone want to kill her?"

"I don't know. It still doesn't sit right with me. That money had to come from somewhere. Unless you thought the telly and computer were more valuable than they are. And it could have been an old ticket."

Fi bit her lip. "No, definitely not. They were expensive. Marty knows a lot about technology. And I'm nearly certain the date on that ticket said this year. It was dated a few weeks from now."

Granny Coyle baulked. "It doesn't sound like her. The only time I've ever seen a smile on her face was when she was bragging about going off to America. It surprises me that she missed an opportunity to let us know about it."

"She obviously didn't want anyone to know."

"But why?"

It was at that point that Fiona seemed to hit a brick wall. She sat back down and clasped both her hands around her cup of now-tepid tea. "It doesn't really matter, does it? She had all that stuff—so what? It doesn't bring us any closer to finding out what happened." She glanced at the untidy pile of pages on the table. "I'm sorry, Granny. I shouldn't have put ideas into your head. What if the sergeant had come in and caught you photocopying his paperwork? I should never have said a thing."

Rose's eyebrows shot up so high they were in danger of disappearing into her hairline. "You're sorry for *putting ideas into my head*? Good Lord, girl, what do you think I am, an impressionable little thing? Some sweet old dear who spends her days making jam and being conned left, right and centre by anyone who sets out to pull the wool over her eyes?"

"No," Fi said warily. "No, I don't think that at all. I just feel guilty for getting you into this mess. What if the sergeant finds out you copied these files? It's a serious offence."

"You didn't get me into this mess," Rose said stonily. "Do you think it was your curiosity that drove me to lace your man's coffee and figure out how to photocopy a load of papers in the time it took him to go and do his business?"

"Um… yeah?"

"Oh of course it wasn't, you silly yoke you. Sure haven't I been listening to you and your brothers come up with all kinds of schemes over the years? I should think I'm immune to it by now. No, love, I did it for my daughter."

"For Mam?"

"Of course. We have our ups and downs, but she's still my daughter. And God knows this thing has her all riled up. If I can get to the bottom of it and see the real killer put away… well, let's just say I miss your mother hounding me about slowing down and taking things easy at my age. I just want to go back to fighting about silly things, not worrying about her stressing over this business."

Fiona shook her head. "I've been worried too."

Granny Coyle didn't look surprised. "I had a look through these papers as I was feeding them through the copier. And it seems to me that the guards have hit a dead end. They've got nothing."

"Neither do we."

"We have each other. And we have a bigger incentive. Sure, Brennan might have the promise of a bonus or a gold star on his record, but we've got your mother's liberty and sanity to think of. That should give us a head-start."

"But I've got nothing," Fiona sighed, desperately trying and failing to find something valuable in everything they had learnt that morning.

"Did Mrs Roche get back to you about meeting for a chat?"

Rose shook her head. "No. I haven't heard back from her. It's not like her."

Fi sighed. She was officially out of ideas.

"Don't give up! You did great work finding poor Declan Hanlon's murderer."

"That was different. It was obvious once all the pieces came together, and it wasn't just me. I don't know. There's nothing here. Nothing. She had no enemies. No friends that we know of. It's like her whole life was secret; hidden from the people here. Like where did she get that big flash telly and computer? She didn't drive. She never took the bus anywhere and there's nowhere to get stuff that hi-tech in Ballycashel. She's a mystery."

"Ah," Rose said with a wave of her hand. "Where's the mystery there? She probably got it all on the internet."

"But there was no record in her bank statements."

"Gift cards? You can buy them anywhere. Maybe someone sent them to her. A niece or nephew."

"For thousands of euro?"

"They could be well off. You never know."

Fiona started to nod, but then she froze as a thought struck her. "The internet," she muttered. "That flash new computer. That's it!"

Rose frowned. "I don't think so, love. They can't have killed her to take her computer. Didn't they smash it and leave it there?"

"No," Fiona said, jumping to her feet. "No, that's not what I meant. Think about it. She had this big flash machine. She must have spent a lot of time online to warrant such a luxury purchase. You suspected as much yourself."

"You're right," Rose said. "But it's broken now so I suppose we'll never know."

Fi shook her head. "Not necessarily."

"Where do you think you're going in such a hurry? We need to stick at it if we have any hope of figuring this out."

"No," Fi said. "We need to get over there. Maybe the clue to who killed her is on that computer. I've got to get over and have a look."

"But it's broken!"

"If the data's any way retrievable, Marty'll be able to get at it."

"Well I'm coming too, then."

134

"Oh come on, Granny. I'm not going to have you arrested for breaking and entering."

"I won't be. Come on. You promised me you'd involve me in this, no matter how risky. Now, I'm coming with you or I'm going over there on my own. Got it?"

"Granny…"

"Don't you *granny* me. Now, come on. The sooner we get over there, the sooner we'll find out if it can be saved."

"I'VE NEVER SEEN you walk so fast. Are you sure you don't want to pop round to Mam and Dad's house and get the car?"

"No, I do not," Rose said, not slowing her pace in the slightest. "If we go there we'll only stop for tea and a snack and it'll delay us. We don't have the time. The last thing we want is some long-lost relative coming out of the woodwork and going in to have a root through Mrs Stanley's belongings. We need to get there fast."

"Long-lost relatives..." Fiona said, trying to remember if she'd ever heard about relatives coming to town to visit Mrs Stanley. "Does she have any relations living nearby?"

"Not that I know of. But the thing about some

relatives is you don't see them at all when you're alive. These people only come sniffing around when they hear you're gone."

Fi winced. "I can't imagine how anyone could be so sneaky."

"Well, you might have a different attitude when you get to my age and see it happen with your own eyes. Never underestimate how much money can change a person." She slowed and stared at the Miller house. "Oh look. There's a fire going. They must have finally sold that place. That's good to see after all the trouble they had."

"Mmm," was all Fiona could manage to say, because she was thinking of the new occupant and not the strangeness of her granny's statement. She had never heard of any trouble at the Miller house.

Her response made Rose instantly suspicious.

"You've gone awful quiet. Do you know something?"

She shrugged. "I met the guy who's renting it. It's actually a friend of Colm's. Angus. I've met him before." She tried to sound as casual as she could, but she could hear the tension in her own voice.

"Is that so?"

"Yeah." *Keep talking,* Fiona told herself. *She'll get suspicious otherwise.* "A friend of Colm's."

"So you've said."

KATHY CRANSTON

They walked on in silence with Fiona frantically trying to think of something to say to change the subject. The ideas should have been leaping off her tongue with everything that had happened recently, but she found herself completely at a loss for something to say.

"I take it he's an attractive young man from the way you seem to have lost your ability to string two words together."

"I was thinking about the case, Granny," Fiona said in a pious voice despite the fact that she was lying through her teeth.

"You're lying through your teeth."

Fiona sighed. "Okay, maybe so. But only to get you to stop harassing me. Can we focus on solving this thing?"

Finally, Rose grunted. "Fine. But I'll be expecting a full report as soon as we've solved this thing and our murderer is behind bars."

"Deal," Fiona said, wishing she felt as confident as her granny sounded. In her mind, they were as far from solving the case as they had been the moment she got that frantic call from Ben.

"AH FIONA," Rose said a few minutes later when

they'd snuck through the broken window at the back of Mrs Stanley's house. Fiona had been alarmed to see it—she felt sure that the guards would have boarded it up or otherwise secured it. The crime scene tape fluttered limply nearby.

But the neglected window was the least of her worries, it appeared.

"I don't understand. It was right here," she said, pointing to the empty top of the desk. There were various trinkets and souvenirs from Fort Lauderdale around it Fiona saw now, but no computer.

"Really?"

"There's no need to sound so sceptical. Look, there's the keyboard and mouse. Why would she have those if she didn't have a computer? And why would anyone take it? It was broken."

"I don't know," Rose said with a long weary sigh. "Maybe for the same reason as you want it."

Desperately, Fiona looked around. "Maybe the guards realised there might be something valuable on there and took it away since we were last here."

Rose shook her head. "Hardly. We'd have seen it on the reports. And I was there this morning. They weren't doing anything except for sitting on their cushioned behinds and ploughing into the coffee."

"I don't get it. It was here. I know it was." She

turned, waving her hands in excitement. "Unless somebody broke in."

"We know somebody broke in. Two people. Remember? Alan Power was here after you."

"No," Fiona said. "No, somebody else. We saw *him*. He was on foot and he was carrying a box under his arm. No, someone must have broken in since then."

Rose said nothing. The strange reproachful look on her face confused Fiona for a few moments, until she followed her grandmother's gaze to the mantle.

"Oh," she whispered.

"Oh, indeed."

The flat-screen TV was still in its place, disproving Fiona's theory in an instant. She walked over to it and carefully pulled it.

"What on earth are you doing girl?"

Fi turned back. "Seeing if it's glued on there. That might explain the thieves leaving it behind. It's not though."

"It just doesn't make sense." Fiona slumped down in an overstuffed armchair that looked like it had been in service since the fifties, before leaping to her feet when she thought better of making herself at home in a dead woman's house.

"It depends on how you look at it," Rose sighed, looking around. "I wonder if she has any teabags.

Knowing her, she probably has the own-brand kind and not the good stuff."

"Granny," Fi cried, wincing. "We're not here to have a little tea party. There's no way I'm making myself a cuppa here."

"Speak for yourself. I'd kill for a lovely strong cup of tea."

"The only one you'd kill is yourself—or do you not remember how Mrs Stanley met her end? For all we know, all the cups in the house have been laced with poison just in case she didn't eat enough of her fry."

Rose hastily stopped rummaging around in the kitchen.

"Right. What do we do now? It's obvious we're not going to find anything useful here."

"Is it?" Rose asked with a twinkle in her eye.

"Well, yeah. The computer's gone. That's what we came here for."

Rose smiled. "Think about it, Fiona. It was here the other day when you came and it's not here now. We've already established that nobody's broken in here looking for valuables, or else that big telly would be gone. So." She pursed her lips. "Who's been in here in the meantime?"

"Alan Power," Fi said immediately. "But he…" She shook her head, trying to remember what she'd seen that night. It was possible that he'd had a computer under his arm: she hadn't seen exactly what he was carrying. "Why would he take her computer? It was all smashed up. And he works in IT. I don't see how it's of any value to him."

"So it's not the computer itself," Rose said, eyes sparkling. "But what's on it."

"But why?" Fiona cried, too frustrated to even think of keeping her voice down. "What could be on it? And how would he even know about it, even if she had had thousands of euro in Bitcoin or what have you." Her eyes lit up. "Maybe that's it. Maybe that's where her money was kept and how she's been able to buy all this stuff."

"I don't know. I get the feeling that she came into money recently and she wasn't keen to let anyone around here know it. I certainly can't see her telling a young man who's just recently moved to town. She can't have had any dealings with him."

"Unless," Fi whispered. "Unless… He's an IT expert, right? Maybe she was having trouble setting all this stuff up and she knew where he worked. You said she was sharp; that she knew how to approach you when she wanted something. He could have come over, seen the Bitcoin account or what have you, and decided he wanted it for himself."

"Maybe. It sounds a little far-fetched, don't you think?"

Fiona nodded. "It sounds a *lot* far-fetched. It doesn't sound like him at all, does it? He's always kept himself to himself and he's never taken part in any of the community work events in the town or volunteered to help out at the pensioner's party or anything like that. Can you see him taking the time to help her set up her computer?"

"There's only one way to find out," Rose said, eyes twinkling. "I think I'll give him a call later on and see if he'll help out an old dear who's having troubles with the aul interwebs."

Fi rolled her eyes. Her granny was more IT literate than she was. Fi suspected she spent her evenings playing online poker, but she'd never been able to prove it and Granny Coyle wasn't letting on.

"Hold off," Fi said, shivering. "So we have a theory about Powers and what he was doing there. What about the murderer? We still don't have any idea who poisoned her."

"Let's solve one riddle at a time," Rose said at last. "There's no point in us standing here—we're only running the risk of getting caught by the guards. We'll go. You can make the tea and I'll give Alan Power a call; test his patience for doing an old lady a kindness."

1 9

Fiona got the kettle on as her granny settled back in the snug and called around to get hold of Alan Power's mobile number. Fi expected they'd be calling around for quite a while, but by the time she arrived at the table with a tray of tea things, Rose was sitting back looking triumphant.

"I got it," she announced.

"Already? How'd you do that?"

"Old Johnnie who used to be the postman. Has a real eye for numbers, that fella. Anyone who ever got a parcel delivered where the mobile was required, he'd take one glance at it and there you go, he'd remember the number from there on out. You should ask him—go and ask him your number and see what he tells you."

"But I already know my number," Fi said with a shrug.

Rose rolled her eyes. "That wasn't my point. It's a skill. Those are dying out these days with the internet and everyone stuck on their phones. Who needs to remember a number when it's all kept in there for you?"

"It's handy."

"It is, but it's ruining peoples' memories. That's all I'm saying. Anyway. He gave me Alan Power's number and I have it written down here." She held up one of Fi's matchbooks with a neatly-written line of digits jotted down on the inside. "I also asked him about delivering parcels to Mrs Stanley."

"You did? What did he tell you?"

"Not much, I'm afraid. He'd deliver the odd letter here and there, mostly from America. He retired three years ago now, though, so well before her current shopping spree."

Fiona sighed. She'd expected there to be something else; something significant that might point them in the right direction.

As Rose made the call to Power, Fiona stood again and moved back to the bar, thinking she might as well do something useful and get ready for that evening's trade.

Guilt welled up in her again at the thought that

she was letting her business fall by the wayside as she focused all her time and energy on the murder case. She shook her head and busied herself cleaning down the bar counter. After all, it wasn't like murders were two a penny in Ballycashel. Now that there'd been two in a relatively short amount of time, it was probably safe to say that things would calm down and there wouldn't be another person killed for a very long time.

At least, she hoped so.

She fell into a familiar routine, spraying and wiping, spraying and wiping. Not that the counter was dirty, but it gave her satisfaction to know that the place was pristine. She moved onto the kitchen behind the bar next, working her way along all the counters and food preparation areas.

"Well I spoke to him," Rose bellowed from back in the bar.

All thoughts of cleanliness evaporated from Fiona's mind. She threw down her cloth and pulled off her gloves as she hurried back to the snug.

"Well? What did he say?"

Rose's eyes sparkled. "Oh, he was quite dismissive. Where did I come across his number and he was sorry if I'd gotten the wrong end of the stick, but he's a working professional not a computer teacher. He's got a very important job and certainly doesn't have time to come to help me get to grips with technology. If I need help, they run courses for the elderly in the library once a month. He sounds like a remarkably unpleasant fellow, but that's good for our purposes, isn't it? At least we know without a shadow of a doubt that he wasn't over at her house for—"

"Wait!" Fiona cried. "What did you just say?"

Rose frowned. "You need me to repeat all that? Were you not listening?" She sighed, as if she'd been slighted. "I suppose I can tell you again. Wait 'til I see. I asked him if it was possible at all that he might come over and help me get my computer connected to the online. Of course it pained me to go on as if I knew nothing about it, but I thought it was the best approach. Anyway, he said—"

"No, Granny. The bit about the library."

"Oh. Apparently there are computer classes there once a month. He didn't lower himself to tell me when, but I imagine the details are on the internet if you want them. Though he did say they were aimed at the elderly—you should have heard the way he said it. So dismissive. Ah, he'll be old himself one day. Hah, he'll regret it then."

Fiona shook her head. "No, not the classes. Just…" She picked up her phone and searched, not expecting to find anything. She was surprised.

Ballycashel library had a basic-looking website but it contained all the information anyone could ever hope to know about a small-town library. The classes were held on the first Saturday morning of every month. She closed her eyes. Her mother had had her run-in with Mrs Stanley on Tuesday. So she couldn't have been there for class. Fi scrolled down through the events page and couldn't find any reference to any classes on Tuesday mornings.

"What was she doing at the computers in the library?" she whispered. "She had a perfectly good setup at home. Those library computers are ancient; big old blocks of things. Hers was a top end all-in-one model."

Rose shook her head. "It certainly sounds odd."

"More than odd. Remember, Mam said Mrs Stanley was on the computer in the library. Whatever Mam caught sight of made Mrs Stanley hurry away. Granny," Fi said, eyes lighting up. "I think we might be on to something!"

"Oh."

The library was almost empty at this time of day, but that wasn't enough to comfort Fiona. She thought it was going to be an easy matter of asking someone nicely to get out of the way while they did a quick check of the history on the two computers.

She hadn't banked on there being ten computers to choose from.

"I thought they only had two," she hissed, earning herself a filthy look from Jean the librarian.

"They used to. Then the school donated the machines from their old computer lab. Most of them sit unused but Jean saw no sense in looking a gift horse in the mouth."

"That's great," Fi said without enthusiasm. "But it doesn't help us, does it? I'll go get Mam."

"No," Rose hissed. "If she comes down here and sees me, she's going to know immediately that we're up to something."

"What do you suggest then? That we go through the history for each of these? It'll take us ages."

"You're right. But we can't get her down here."

"Wait, I have an idea."

A moment later, Fi was outside, listening to dial tone and waiting for her mother to answer the phone.

"Mam, it's Fi. Listen, do you remember which computer Mrs Stanley was at before you had the altercation in the street." She squeezed her eyes shut and waited for the onslaught.

Sure enough, Margaret McCabe was less than impressed at being reminded of her indecorous conduct. "What are you asking me that for, Fiona? Can I not just be allowed to forget the whole thing? I'll have you know she was up to something. What was I supposed to do? I'm not a saint, Fiona. Lord knows, I have the patience of one at times, but I'm not. What do you think I'm—"

"Mam," Fi said, trying to inject a soothing tone into her voice. "Mam, I'm not having a go at you. Listen." She thought fast. "I'm at the library now and I thought I'd go in and clean the computer of any record of that picture of you."

Margaret hesitated. "You can do that? So my picture is on there?"

"I don't know," Fi whispered. It was easy to lead her mother up the garden path because when it came to computers, Margaret really didn't have a clue. Nor did she have any interest in learning. "Look, it'll save you doing it and it'll only take a minute, but I need to make sure I get the right one."

Margaret made a strange groaning sound.

"Mam, are you alright?"

"Shush, I'm thinking."

She made the noise again. It was very disconcerting, especially when it was your mother and you were hearing this on the phone. Fiona was about to ask her if she couldn't just think silently, but she held back.

Finally, Margaret grunted. "It was the one at the back, closest to the shelves."

"At the back, Mam?" Fiona asked, poking her head in the door and looking to see where her mother meant. "You mean not one of the ones facing the door?"

"Oh no, of course not. She was hidden at the back there, closest to the shelves. Probably thinking no one would discover her there, the little snake—Lord have mercy on her. I wouldn't have had any cause to go anywhere near her if I hadn't been looking for a book about local poets for the poetry week we're looking at setting up."

"Thanks, Mam," Fi said, eager to get in there and see for herself.

"You'll make sure it's cleaned."

"I will."

"And are you over for your dinner tonight? I have gammon in the oven. And there's stew in the fridge if you're home before it's ready."

Her mouth watered at the prospect. Her mother always overdid it so the joint of meat stuck to the bottom of the glass dish. If you got in there early, you got to eat the bit at the bottom, all caramelized and deliciously salty-sweet. She shook her head—now wasn't the time to be thinking about food.

"I don't know yet, Mam. I'll buzz you later, okay?"

She didn't wait to hear the response. She hung up and put the phone back in her jacket pocket before re-entering the library. Jean was a real stickler for rules—that was probably the reason why Fiona hadn't been in there in years.

She hurried across the floor to where Rose was standing close to the computers.

"Stand back," Fiona whispered, nodding her head at Mrs Flannery, who was sitting at the machine closest to them. "Give her some privacy."

"We might need it," Rose said at her normal volume. "She's only looking at rubbishy clothes to buy anyway."

Fiona grabbed her grandmother's arm and hurried over to the other side of the bank of desks, not missing the filthy look Mrs Flannery threw the two of them. "Keep your voice down! Anyway, it's not that one. Mam told me it was that one over there beside the shelves. More out of the way."

"But sure anyone could sneak up behind you there."

Fiona wandered over and pulled out a few of the books from the shelf nearest the vacant computer. "I don't think so," she said, holding up an ancient copy of Amateur Poetry Annual. "I can't imagine there's much demand for this stuff."

The whole shelf was filled with similar titles, none of which looked like they'd been moved in years, if the thick layer of dust on the shelf was anything to go by.

"No, she had a nice little private spot for herself here. She must have got a right shock when Mam started shouting at her."

"I'll say."

Fi pulled the chair out and sat down. It was only then that she noticed the little wooden divider that separated this desk from the ones beside it, which were more open. "Look at this. She had a very private area. Why did she need it? She had all the privacy in the world in her own house."

"Let's find out."

They turned on the machine and waited for it to boot up, which seemed to take forever. Finally, an outdated operating system that Fi hadn't seen for years appeared. It took her a few minutes to get the hang of the unfamiliar layout. She half expected to have to start a dialup connection, but the little symbol appeared in the bottom corner telling her she was connected. She opened a browser window and stared at it.

"You'll want to bring up the history," Rose

prompted. "Let's see. Was it Tuesday morning that Margaret had her run-in with Mrs Stanley?"

Fiona nodded, clicking on the history button and waiting for it to load. For an awful second she thought it might be set up not to keep a record, but a second later a long list of websites appeared.

She scrolled to the bottom of the list and selected the option to look at the past seven days' worth of history. There wasn't that much activity on there, so it didn't take long for them to find Tuesday's. In fact, all of the timestamps appeared to be in the same half hour window.

"Wow," Fiona said, unable to believe what she was seeing. "Mrs Stanley may have been the only person to use this computer that day. We're in luck."

Rose leaned forward over her shoulder to read the list. "Are we? I don't see anything on there that's incriminating."

Fiona skimmed through the list and saw what she meant. Apart from Facebook, Mrs Stanley had looked at a travel website, Gmail and the parish council site, just as Margaret had claimed. Fi didn't know what she'd expected to see, but she'd assumed there'd be something.

She clicked the link and was faced with a page describing prominent volunteers in the parish. Her mother's picture was on there. Her heart sank.

"Do you think this was what she meant? If that's the case, then maybe Mrs Stanley was only looking through the page."

"No," Rose said. "Remember. Margaret was sure she was doing something with it. It wasn't the parish website. She was sure it was Facebook."

Fiona clicked the link, hoping Mrs Stanley had forgotten to log out in her rush to get away.

No such luck.

She sighed. "Well, even if it was some sort of profile, we'll never know now. She logged out, or the system logged her out. It doesn't much matter what happened—we can't get in without her password and we don't even know what her username is."

"Let me sit down there for a sec."

Fiona stood and stepped off to the side. She watched, not really paying attention to what her granny was doing. After all, they'd seen all there was to see, hadn't they?

When she glanced at the screen a few moments later, she noticed something odd. Rose's hand was flying around with the mouse, opening all of the links that Mrs Stanley had accessed on Tuesday. When she opened the Gmail one, she let out a satisfied sigh.

"There we go. There's her email address."

"It's locked, though. You need her password to continue."

"We do," Rose said thoughtfully. "Anyway." She clicked back to the window with Facebook open and typed Mrs Stanley's email address into the email field.

Fiona was about to object when she realised there was no harm in trying. She struggled to maintain her focus, though—after all, it was a pointless exercise. She looked around the library, wondering how it managed to stay open when it was so quiet. Maybe it was busier on the weekends, she thought. Whatever the reason, she thought she'd been a little slack in not going there for so long. They seemed to have a good selection of newish releases in the shelf closest to the door, and there were also several comfy-looking armchairs spread around the place. It certainly looked more comfortable than her flat. She had half a mind to come here next time she needed to dedicate a morning to doing her books.

She looked over at Jean, about to ask her when the library had got in the new chairs—last she remembered, they'd had those awful moulded plastic ones she couldn't stand.

She soon forgot about chairs when her eyes landed on the screen.

"You got in? What the hell?"

They were looking at what appeared to be Mrs Stanley's newsfeed.

Rose swivelled around to face her with a big smile on her face. "Some people are diligent with their passwords, but the vast majority pick something really obvious like 'password' or 1234567890'. I read an article about it. Now, others think they're being crafty by putting in the name of a loved one or a pet, but it's only slightly harder to guess."

Fiona shook her head in utter disbelief. "You guessed her password?"

"I tried a few times," Rose said nodding. "I'll admit I was a bit stumped when her maiden name didn't work, or Glenbeg, her townsland. But then I typed in Fort Lauderdale and it let me in!"

"Great work, Granny! Now." Fiona grabbed the chair from the nearest computer and pulled it over beside Rose's. "Let's find out what she had to hide. It must have been something big to bring her all the way here. What could she have done here that she couldn't have done at home?"

THE NEWSFEED OFFERED FEW CLUES. There were no upcoming events and it didn't appear that Mrs Stanley had posted anything in months. The few posts she had made were shares of uncontroversial animal videos. She had about forty friends, very few of whom Fiona recognised.

"Check her messages," Fi said, before second-guessing the ethics of that. Was it a step too far?

It was too late. Rose had clicked the little message link on the top menu.

Fiona let out a sigh—she hadn't realised up to that point that she'd been holding her breath.

"There's nothing. Literally a handful of messages from about a year ago."

The disappointment was so great that it seemed

to swirl around Fi. It really had seemed like they were on to something. If it wasn't for her mother's story about catching Mrs Stanley in the middle of something, she would have given up and gone home.

"Mam saw something. She must have—it's just not like her to have a fight with another woman in the middle of the street."

Rose shook her head. "But there's nothing in here. It doesn't look like she's done anything on here for months."

Fi bit her lip. "Will we try her email? For all Mam knew, maybe she was sending that picture to someone in an email."

"I can try." Rose was already opening another window and going to Gmail. "With a bit of luck she's got the same password."

This time, Fiona couldn't look away. She felt a little burst of triumph when it became clear that Mrs Stanley's inbox was loading, but that feeling disappeared when the list of emails appeared and she scanned through their subjects and senders.

"These are mostly order confirmations from online retailers."

"There might be something further down." Rose scrolled slowly through the list, but there was nothing remarkable there. There was one email from her sister but aside from that, nothing. The sent items folder was even more barren, with only a reply to her sister, which the date stamp said had been sent six weeks before.

"I guess that's our theory out the window," Fiona said, shaking her head. There was nothing more they could do—they had checked all the sites Mrs Stanley had accessed. There was no picture of Margaret McCabe anywhere.

"I hope your mother wasn't having some kind of episode," Rose said gravely.

"No, of course not. She's mad but not like that. We'd have known."

"But there's nothing! Nothing at all that explains why someone would want to kill her." Rose sighed and logged out of Mrs Stanley's email account. "I'll just check my own emails and then we'll head away. It's getting on and neither of us has eaten for hours."

Fiona became aware of her own hunger at that point and her stomach rumbled in response. She was just about to suggest going across the road to the bakery when she saw what was on the screen.

"Granny!" Fi burst forward, grabbing Rose's arm before she could click away from the page she was on. "Those names!"

"What names, love? Those? Oh, they're just the email addresses that have been accessed from this machine. See? I need to click down here to add my own email address and log in."

Fiona stared at the screen. She knew that—she'd been seeing the same screen since she set up a new account for her bar: she always had to select whether she wanted her own personal email account or the one for McCabe's. Now they were looking at a list of three email addresses that had been accessed on this computer.

"They're probably someone else's."

Fiona shook her head. Goosebumps prickled on her skin as she got the overwhelming feeling that this was it; this was the lead they were looking for.

"No. Look, that's Eunice Doyle at Gmail dot com. There's Mrs Stanley's. But who's this?"

Rose shook her head. "Pete Smith at Gmail dot com. I don't know. Maybe one of the people from the new estate."

It was still called the new estate around the town even though the houses had been finished for more than ten years.

"No, Granny. I don't know anyone by that name in town. And even if you don't know people, you'd have heard of them."

Rose shrugged. "It could be an out-of-towner."

"Really? In the library?"

"A Spanish student."

"With a name like Pete Smith? If anything it sounds like an alias."

"You're right!" Rose exclaimed, earning a warning look from Jean, not that she noticed. She clicked the mouse and her hands flew across the keyboard as she tried to work out the password.

"It worked! You were right!" Rose was too excited to keep her voice down. "She used the same password for everything, the fool."

"Granny, shhh. We need privacy for this."

Rose looked around, saw Jean and nodded. "Okay," she said in a loud whisper. "Right, we're in. Let's see what we can find here."

A bunch of spammy-looking emails, as it turned out.

Fiona shook her head. "I don't get it. This is obviously hers. She went to the trouble of making up a name and it must be her account if the password is the same. So why aren't we seeing anything? This is all just..." she read the subject line of one of the emails, proclaiming to be able to cure all kinds of ailments... "It's just junk."

"You're right about that," Rose said, clicking into the sent items.

They were both surprised to see a completely blank folder.

"There's nothing? No sent items?"

Rose nodded. "It looks that way. What about here?"

The promotions tab was full of similar junk to the inbox. Fiona was about to give up when her granny opened the 'social' tab. She gasped, unable to believe what she was seeing.

"Look at that! Look at all those updates from Facebook." She leaned forward to get a closer look. "And those names. Look, it's Trish Mahony." The subject line saw 'new message from Louise Graham'. Further down, past a few notifications about people commenting on stuff, there was another message entitled 'new message from James Brady'. "What's going on, Granny? I recognise those names. They live here in Ballycashel."

"They do," Rose said gravely. "What was she at using an alias? Maybe we're wrong and these are people with the same names as locals here. But it still doesn't make sense."

They opened the top email, which had been sent the week before. It showed a message from Trish Mahony and Fiona felt a jolt of recognition when she saw the picture. It was definitely the Trish Mahony who lived in Ballycashel—there she was in the picture with her beloved golden retriever.

"What do you think it means?"

Fiona shook her head. The message was short and

appeared to be a reply to a previous message, which wasn't visible. All it said was 'how do I know that'll be the end of it?'

"Click on that link; the one that says 'view conversation on Facebook'," Fiona whispered.

Rose clicked and the Facebook login page came up. Quick as a flash, she typed in the fake email address and the same password. Seconds later, the screen refreshed with a red field. Wrong password.

"Huh. We'll try something else."

But it was no use. Rose used everything she knew about Mrs Stanley to try and get in, but nothing worked.

"I don't understand it," Rose said. "Why would she have a different password for this one? What's so special about it?"

"This must be it," Fiona said with a sinking feeling. "This is what she was killed for. And we can't access it."

"We can try again in a while with a different password."

"What password? We've tried everything."

"Well... we could find out her wedding anniversary from the parish register."

Fiona sighed. It seemed like a much less promising option now that Mrs Stanley had gone to the trouble to choose a hard-to-guess password for this particular account.

"Let's go back to her email. Maybe we can piece it together from there."

Fiona ran to the counter and asked for a pen and paper, which Jean handed over begrudgingly. She had half a mind to tell her that they were doing important work, but she held her tongue. Knowing Jean, she'd be on the phone to Sergeant Brennan within seconds.

There wasn't a lot of information to be had from Mrs Stanley's secret Gmail account, but they did manage to find a bit. In all, there were conversations with eight Ballycashel locals. There was one email from weeks before saying "Alan Power sent you a message'—the body of that email gave no clue as to the message's contents and there was no further notification of messages in the chain.

That in itself was strange.

"What do you think," Fiona asked, pointing to the screen. "Isn't it funny that there were no more responses?"

Granny Coyle shook her head. "I don't know. It's hard to know when we can't see the messages she sent herself. What does all this tell us?"

"I don't know."

They'd read all the messages that formed part of Facebook conversations and none of them revealed anything much. There was a common thread to them, however: all of them seemed to be frightened of something. A few of them begged Mrs Stanley to leave them alone. That just confused them even more.

"She was small and frail. She was hardly able to walk, for God's sake! Why were they so afraid of her?"

Fiona shook her head. A thought had cropped into her mind but it was so ridiculous she hesitated to share it out loud.

"Go on. You have that faraway look in your eyes."

She sighed. "Okay, but it's pretty out-there."

"Isn't it all?"

"Right. Well. What if it was some sort of blackmail? That email from Trish. It seemed to be looking for reassurance that this was the end of it. What if she had something on all of these people and she was using that knowledge to extort money out of them?"

"It seems possible. But what?"

Fiona shrugged. "I don't know. It was just a thought. Okay, I've written down all the names. We've got Jimmy Brady, Trish Mahony, Louise Graham, Alan Power, Bernard Boyle and Mrs Roche.

None of their messages really go into detail, but they were all pleading with Mrs Stanley in one way or another. So I guess we've got some more suspects. Wait, do you think this is why Mrs Roche never got back to you?"

"What are you asking, Fiona?" her granny demanded.

Fi shrugged sheepishly. Rose and Agnes Roche were good friends. She resolved to do some subtle digging when she was alone. "Nothing."

"Do you know what I'm just after thinking of? Your mother hardly ever goes online, does she? God knows, I'm always at her to brush up on her skills. She doesn't even know how to get on her online banking and it's often cheaper that way."

"She doesn't trust it."

"Neither do I," Rose said gruffly. "But that's neither here nor there. She has Facebook, though, doesn't she? I'm sure I added her as a friend. Supposing she has a message from this Pete Smith fella too and she just hasn't seen it? It might explain what Mrs Stanley was up to in the library that morning. And I can't imagine Margaret would have kept it to herself if she received something like that."

Fiona smirked. "We set her up on it because she was complaining about missing out but then she hardly used it after. I'm not sure she even remembers. I think you could be on to something!"

"Let's go!" Rose exclaimed, standing up with a flourish and earning another filthy look from Jean. "We finally have a lead to follow!"

"Wait," Fiona said, holding up her hands in protest.

They had barely made it as far as the crossroads, but she couldn't go on any longer.

"What is it?" Rose asked, seeming genuinely perplexed.

"Aren't you starving? We haven't eaten. You said…"

"Ah. I suppose I did. I got carried away with solving the case. We'll eat soon."

"I can't wait."

"But we're going to your mother's. She'll feed us."

"It'll take us, what, ten minutes to get there. I'll just grab a chicken fillet roll."

"You'll do no such thing," Rose said, taking her

arm with surprising force. "What would your poor mother think if I let you eat aul deli food?"

"She'd thank you for not letting me starve?" Fiona said weakly.

The hunger had hit her suddenly, but now it was on her mind it wasn't going away. Her stomach ached from emptiness and her hands were starting to shake from the lack of fuel.

"I need to eat something."

"Come on so," Rose said. "We'd better hurry up."

Fiona was fit to collapse by the time they arrived at her parents' house. Not only that, but hunger had segued into hanger, and she felt fit to bite the head off anyone that looked crooked at her.

At that moment, Marty was the poor unfortunate who was sitting in her path.

"Where were you when we needed you, hah?"

He looked up from a hearty plate of stew and mashed potato, clearly confused. "Mwaphmph?"

"Martin McCabe," his mother barked, emerging from the kitchen. "I'll thank you not to speak with your mouth full."

"Sorry Mam, she surprised me." He turned to Fiona and frowned. "I don't know why you're on your high horse. I was at work. Running the shop. We can't all gallivant around the place all day."

Guilt shot through Fiona, making her forget her hunger for a moment. "We're trying to figure out who…" she trailed off, remembering her mother was in the room.

"Don't mind him, love," Rose said, shooting her a warning look. "Most of your trade is at night. Sure it was only silly opening during the day. You're not a cafe, you're a bar. And you." She turned to Marty. "Don't let her rise you. You know she gets like a demon when she's hungry."

"I do not!"

"Point proven."

"Margaret, would you please get some food into this girl's throat before she goes off the deep end. Please."

Harmony was restored just a few minutes later, after Fiona had wolfed down an overflowing bowl of stew. She looked up to find her grandmother watching her intently.

"Are we feeling human again?"

Fi couldn't help but smile. It was a running joke in the family that she would be fine one minute and then utterly famished the next. She had theorised that it was down to her having a fast metabolism— her sister Kate had soon disabused her of that notion, rolling her eyes and announcing that fast metabolisms and bingo wings rarely came in the same package.

"Much better, thanks. I hadn't eaten for hours."

"Right," Rose announced, all business again. "Margaret, we need to ask you something."

"What, Mammy. You sound very… serious."

"It's serious enough alright. Fiona tells me you have Facebook."

Margaret McCabe looked confused for a moment before something seemed to dawn on her. "Yes, yes you're right. Ben got it for me a while ago."

"When's the last time you signed in, Mam?"

Margaret shook her head. "I couldn't tell you. Sure I went on and had a look, and to be honest it didn't interest me in the slightest."

"Can you show us your profile?" Granny Coyle asked authoritatively.

"My what now?"

"Your profile. Show us your Facebook." There was a real impatience in Granny Coyle's tone now, and Fiona didn't like it one bit. She got the feeling there were things about the case they hadn't told her and suspected that her mother was more at risk than Rose had let on.

"It's on the computer. In there in Francis's study."

That was how they referred to the front room,

which most people used as a dining room. Because the kitchen area was unusually vast and had two dining areas already, Francis had long ago seized the front room and called it his study. He only used it to read his newspaper and get away from his kids, but no-one had thought to try and reclaim it.

They all stood and trooped one-by-one out of the kitchen, along the hall. They came to a stop outside the closed door to the study.

"Go on then," Rose said. "Don't stand on ceremony."

Margaret threw the door open and they came face-to-face with a sleeping Francis McCabe—his newspaper had fallen on the floor beside his chair.

"He's like a big baby," Rose mused, before making a beeline for the computer in the corner.

It was a big ancient thing; the same one as they'd had since Fiona was barely a teenager. Ben and Kate had repeatedly urged their father to upgrade, but that had only made him more resolved to hold onto the old machine—he reasoned that he'd never get a chance to use it if he got a new one that they could commandeer to play games on.

"Right," Rose said, sitting in the chair and waiting as it booted up. "Let's see what's on here."

It took a few minutes, but the beast eventually booted up. It took a couple of goes but they finally deduced that Margaret's password was, in fact, 'Margaret', something that her mother was utterly disgusted by.

"Right," Rose said, matter-of-factly. "This won't take long."

Margaret had ten friends in total, the sum of her efforts on that day Ben had set her up before she completely lost interest. She had fifty friend requests.

"The messages, Granny. Check the messages."

There it was. A message from Pete Smith. Fiona held her breath as her granny clicked on it.

"Oh my."

"What, what is it?"

Fiona turned and held out her hand. Margaret had busied herself dusting the bookshelves, but now she approached them, clearly curious about what was getting her mother and daughter so agitated. "It's nothing, Mam. It's fine."

"I can tell from your tone that it's anything but fine. Let me see."

Fiona tried to stand in the way but it was hopeless. Her mother pushed past her towards the computer. Before she could see what was there, Granny Coyle switched off the monitor.

"It's blank," Margaret huffed. "Turn it back on."

"I think it might have overheated," Rose said. "Anyway, it was nothing."

It took several minutes of back and forth before Margaret was satisfied there was nothing to worry about. When she finally left the room, Francis shook out his newspaper and tutted.

"Overheated me eye."

Granny Coyle shot him a filthy look. "I didn't see you doing anything to stop her. Anyway, it was a white lie. There's no reason for her to see this and get herself all worked up over it. Mrs Stanley is gone now. There's not an earthly thing she can do to your wife."

"Not an earthly thing she could have done before either. Sure she was only a slip of a woman. Margaret's not as easily upset as she makes out."

Fiona glanced at her grandmother. "It wasn't a physical threat she made against Mam."

"What, did she challenge her to a knit-off or something?"

"You ought to take this seriously, Francis."

He coughed. "I don't take anything seriously if it's found on that aul Facebook."

"Well you'd be mistaken."

It must have been the acid in his mother-in-law's tone that made him sit upright and pay attention. A moment later, he was over beside them, turning the monitor back on.

Fiona's stomach plummeted with revulsion when

she saw the message—or, rather, the series of messages.

"Poison pen is an understatement here," she whispered, reading it again. "I'd never have imagined Mrs Stanley was capable of such bile."

"Me neither," Rose said. "And I've known her for longer than most of you have been alive."

"Good God almighty," Francis said when he'd finished reading. "It's a lucky thing Margaret didn't come across this. Anyone else wouldn't pay much heed to such accusations, but she'd be outraged."

That was the thing; there wasn't just one accusation, but many. The first message started off politely enough; a 'hi, how are you' generic sort of message. But from then on, it got ugly.

Pete Smith began to set out Margaret's transgressions. From failing to put money in the church collection envelopes to drinking gin in the daytime, it was a wide-ranging list complete with grainy pictures in some instances. Not only that, but they could all see it was designed to hit Margaret where it hurt: she prided herself on being a good member of the church, one who supported her local parish in any way she could.

It went on and on, finally getting to the real point. Pete Smith wanted five hundred euro to keep quiet. If Margaret didn't give it to him, she'd find her transgressions broadcast on a flyer distributed around the church just in time for eleven o'clock mass on Sunday. She was to put the money in a change bag from the bank and leave it in the empty bucket just inside the gate of Fleming's field.

It was a smart move on Mrs Stanley's part, Fiona thought but dared not say aloud. Fleming's field was close to her house, but there were several other houses in between. There was no way she could be linked to the messages unless someone was to catch her retrieving the money.

But that was the puzzling thing. Those messages had been sent two weeks before the murder, and Mrs McCabe's good name hadn't been destroyed around the parish.

In later messages, it became clear that Mrs Stanley was willing to keep reminding her prey rather than follow through on her threat. There was a new message every few days, urging Margaret to do the right thing soon before it was too late.

The last message—the one sent on the day Mrs Stanley was murdered—was the picture of Margaret from the parish website. The only accompanying text was 'it'll be a shame if they need to find a new member of the council. You know what to do."

"Good God," Francis said again. "Such malice. I'd hate to think what might have happened if she'd survived and Margaret continued to ignore the messages through no fault of her own. Can you imagine? We have to go to the guards."

"No, Dad," Fiona urged, clasping his arm. She'd thought the same thing at first, but having had time to reflect on it, she knew it might backfire.

"What do you mean, 'no'?"

"Well what's Robocop going to think? He's already intent on getting Mam for the murder. All this proves is she had even more of a motive than we already thought."

"But she's the victim. She hasn't even responded or seen the messages!"

"I don't know how we can prove that, though. For all Sergeant Brennan knows, she saw the messages, figured out who was behind them and then bided her time until she could get the threat out of her life—permanently."

"That's crazy."

Fiona shook her head. "The whole thing is crazy. How could someone try and blackmail Mam like that, preying on the things she holds dearest to her? It's obscene."

The door flew open and Fiona gazed in horror at her mother's triumphant expression.

"I knew it!" Margaret McCabe cried. "I knew ye were hiding something from me. I'm no fool."

"We know you're not, Mam. We were just trying to protect you, is all."

"I don't need protecting," she insisted. "I brought you into this world. If anything, I'm the one who should be protecting you."

"And I'd be glad of that if the situation was reversed. I really don't think you should look at..."

It was too late. Margaret had pushed past them and was reading the messages that were still on the screen. Fiona watched in dismay as her mother's face grew redder and redder. When she finally swivelled back to face them, her face was puce.

"That little witch! I've only ever been nice to her and she repays me like this! Setting up a fake name and everything. The gall of that woman!"

Granny Coyle went to her side. "Calm down, Margaret. She's gone now. There's nothing she can do to you."

"Do to me? It's what I'd do to her! I tell you, if she hadn't already been murdered I'd do it myself! She deserved everything that came her way, I can tell you that! The cheek of her! It's lies, absolute lies! As if she'd know how much I put in the envelope for the offertory collection. I'll have you know I wouldn't even consider putting in anything less than ten euro a week. That's at a minimum! And the drinking! That was one time. I'd never usually take a drop until the evening, but to look at that picture you'd think I was an awful wino altogether. Oh, what would people have thought if she'd gone ahead and made her mean little fliers? I can't even imagine…"

"There now, love," Granny Coyle whispered. "It's alright. You mustn't get worked up. She's gone now and it looks as if her wicked little messages are gone with her."

22

"ALL THOSE PEOPLE THEN," Fiona said, her breath coming out as a whistle. "I wonder what she had on them."

Granny Coyle shook her head. "It's not like she even had anything, is it? Margaret said it herself—those accusations were lies and twisted versions of the truth, but she must have counted on the fact that people would believe her claims regardless of whether they were true or not."

"Remember that flyer about two months back? Someone stuck it to lampposts around the town about Jimmy Brady going behind everyone's back and applying to have a wind turbine installed on his land when he'd been one of the most vocal protestors against them. I suppose we know who's behind that now."

"There was a message from Jimmy alright," Fiona said, nodding. "From months back. He said he couldn't afford it. To go easy—he was a hardworking man trying to get by."

"I can't remember any other nasty flyers being put up around the place."

"Everyone else must have paid up."

Francis sighed. "Or resorted to murder to keep Mrs Stanley quiet."

Fiona shivered at the thought. Then she remembered something. "We should go have a look in the barrel at Fleming's field. Just on the off-chance that somebody paid up—we could maybe tie it back to them."

"It's a long shot."

"It's the best we've got," Granny Coyle agreed.

IT WAS INDEED A LONG SHOT. Anticipation had built up in Fiona by the time she and Ben got to the gate, about a twenty walk from their house. Part of her was expecting to find a wad of money with a clue that led them directly to another of Mrs Stanley's victims.

There was nothing. They even climbed over the fence and searched around the bucket, hoping that one of the suspects had dropped something personal near the drop-off point.

"What did you expect?" Ben asked, his voice dripping with sarcasm. "A wad of cash and a business card?"

He had held back from getting involved in their investigation and had only agreed to accompany Fiona because his father had threatened to confiscate the PlayStation.

"No," Fiona said, jamming her hands in the pockets of her jeans.

The truth was she had sort of been expecting something like that; a clear indication of what they needed to do next.

"Right, well there's no reason to be disappointed then. Can we go? I came with you like Dad said. There's no point in us standing around here in the cold."

"It's not cold. It's only September."

He rolled his eyes. "This is Ireland. It's always cold."

"Princess."

"Miss Marple. Why can't you find another hobby —one that isn't an inconvenience to the rest of us?"

She sighed. "You think this is fun for me? I was

curious to begin with, but it's more about getting Mam's name cleared for once and for all."

"Cute. You're such a humanitarian."

"I am not," she muttered, starting to walk back towards the gate. "Why are you so insufferable? I'd understand it if you were a teenager, but you're too old to be behaving like…"

"Well go on," he huffed. "Why stop now. Keep assassinating my character, why don't you."

But she'd stopped listening. Something had caught her eye in the long grass beside the gate. She moved over, cursing herself for losing sight of exactly where it was.

"Fi?"

"Give me a minute," she whispered. "I thought I saw something."

It took a few minutes of rummaging around in the still-damp grass—she was starting to think she'd dreamt it—but then she found it. It was a silver pin that glinted in the weak sunlight.

"What's that?"

She held it up, frowning. "It's a pin from the golf club."

"Let me see."

She handed it to him. Her mind was already working frantically as she tried to piece the puzzle together. What did it mean? Had one of the members of the golf club been targeted by Mrs Stanley or was Mrs Stanley a member herself? She had no idea.

"You haven't had any dealings with the golf club, have you?"

Ben shot her a filthy look. "Of course not. Bunch of snooty aul lads if you ask me."

She was momentarily stumped, until she realised she knew exactly who she could ask.

"THIS IS AN OLD ONE," Francis McCabe said, holding the little badge at arm's length and frowning as he scrutinised it. "Yeah, they changed to plastic a few years ago. I couldn't tell you what year this is from."

Francis had never been a member of the golf club, but he had hosted many of their functions when the clubhouse was being renovated. Donnie, the club's president, had been a regular at McCabe's and he and Francis were still on very friendly terms.

"What do you mean, what year?"

"See up here in the corner? These yokes always have the year in roman numerals. This one's been pawed so much it's rubbed off. The metal ones are much nicer. There was such a hullaballoo when the club made the decision to do plastic ones and save a bit of cash."

"These people have nothing meaningful to complain about," Ben noted bitterly.

"Sure neither do you," Francis said without pausing. "Living here for free and not bothering to go and do an honest day's work. Don't tell me you're working in the hardware shop because I know Marty isn't working you half as hard as he should be. Aren't you meant to be there today? Marty's gone back now after his lunch. He's too soft. Those people—the ones you're so keen to give out about—they're the ones who're paying for your dole."

Fiona smirked.

"Yeah, love. I'd go talk to the secretary about this. He'll be able to tell you what year this is from. He'll possibly even be able to give you a list of members who received one."

"Really? Aren't there hundreds of members?"

Francis nodded. "There are, but as far as I know they don't all buy the new pins every year."

This was encouraging. Fiona couldn't help but feel optimistic about their chances. "Brilliant! Do you have any idea who's the secretary now or should I give Donnie a call?"

"I do. Wait 'til I see." Francis rubbed his chin, frowning. "Ah that's it—I remember reading about the new committee in the paper. It's Bernard Boyle.

He's a lovely man; he won't mind answering a few questions."

Fiona's heart sank. He was a lovely man alright—she'd met him around the town down through the years and he'd even been into her bar a few times. The problem was, she thought, that he might know a bit too much about the case.

"What's the matter, love? You look like you've seen a ghost."

She shook her head. "Dad, Bernard Boyle is one of the people who responded to Mrs Stanley's message."

"No."

"You saw the list yourself. I showed it to you."

"Ah, I was only half paying attention. But now that you mention it again, it doesn't surprise me all that much."

"Why not?"

"Well, there was always something a bit shifty about that fella. I could never put my finger on it, but Mrs Stanley obviously had something on him."

"I suppose," Fi said slowly. "Or it could be like with Mam—she had nothing really, she was just fishing to chance her arm and see if Mam would pay up."

"It could be," Francis said, with a serious

expression that made Fiona very uneasy. "But then again maybe she had something on some people."

Fi threw her hands up in frustration. "We're going round and round in circles here. I keep thinking we've found something useful but then it turns out to be completely unclear. Like now. Is Bernard Boyle just another victim or is there something more sinister going on?"

Her father cleared his throat. "It would seem that he's just a victim. If he paid up—which it seems he did—he might have thought that was the end of it."

"There were several messages back and forth between them. What if she decided she wanted more?"

"We have no way of knowing."

"No," Fiona said, shaking her head. "Not without access to that Facebook profile, we don't. All we can see are the messages she received from her victims. And we have no way of getting into it that I can see. Without it, we've a long list of potential suspects and no way at all of knowing whether they took Mrs Stanley's threats seriously enough to pay up—or worse."

"Oh for God's sake," Kate piped up. She'd been stuck on her phone ever since Fi got back, and she had half-forgotten her sister was even there. "Why don't you just go to the guards? They'll be able to get a warrant for access to the messages."

"She has a point, love," Granny Coyle whispered, squeezing Fiona's arm. "The only way we benefit from investigating this ourselves is if we're making real progress and we're not making progress now. It seems as if we've hit a brick wall. I think it's time we reconsidered getting the guards involved."

Fiona sighed. "I suppose. I'll go get Mam."

23

"Whoa, whoa, whoa," Sergeant Brennan said, holding up his hand. On his wrist was a very shiny watch Fiona had never seen before. She stared at it in disdain, urging herself to stay quiet and not say anything to make him even more sour.

"What?" Margaret McCabe asked, clearly affronted.

He smiled his reptilian smile. "You come in here and tell me a fairy story and then it surprises you when I don't fall for it hook, line and sinker? I must say, you've underestimated me."

"No," Fiona muttered. "I'm not sure that's possible." It was so easy to let a smart comment slip out when you were faced with his hopelessly smug little head.

"Miss McCabe."

"Sergeant Brennan. Apologies if I offended you, but you were being rather dismissive to my mother."

"And we all know you McCabes stick together," he said, sighing as if he was extremely put-upon. "Now, I want you to slow down and tell me what you're trying to say, Mrs McCabe. You're telling me that Mrs Stanley tried to blackmail you."

"Yes," Margaret said, nodding and pulling her cardigan tighter around her. She had been opposed to going to the Garda station at first, and it had taken them over an hour to talk her round. Fiona could see she was growing more agitated and disillusioned by the minute.

Fiona grabbed her hand under the table and squeezed it, hoping her mother would just ignore the sergeant and keep telling her story.

Margaret cleared her throat. "Yes," she said with more certainty. "I didn't see the message at first; not until today. Like I told you, we argued after I saw her on the computer with a picture of me."

He leaned across the desk, eyes narrowed. "And that prompted you to go to her house and poison her breakfast."

"That's clearly not what she was about to say."

"No, indeed," Margaret said with a nod. "No, I only saw those Facebook messages when Fiona asked to get onto my Facebook. I hadn't been on it in months since my son set up my account. It was then that they found the messages from Mrs Stanley."

"And do you have any record of these messages? Am I supposed to take your word for it?" He said this as if the very act of sitting in the room with them was deeply painful for him.

"Here," Fiona said, passing over the pages they had printed out earlier. "This is a printout of the whole conversation."

Beside her, Margaret stiffened. They had tried, but they still hadn't convinced her that Mrs Stanley's accusations against her wouldn't lead to her being arrested. There was no truth in them, and it wasn't a crime to shortchange the offertory collection as long as you weren't stealing from it. They had finally convinced her that the Gardaí wouldn't be able to breathe a word of the accusations, because they had a duty of confidentiality towards their informants (they had made up this last part, but it had done the trick).

"And you promise not to breathe a word of it to anyone."

Sergeant Brennan looked up, seemingly irritated. "If it's evidence, it might be used in court."

"Oh Fiona, I—"

"It's fine, Mammy. Please. Sergeant, it's all there.

She made repeated threats against my mother, saying she'd blacken her name if she didn't pay five hundred euro."

The sergeant sighed but he bowed his head and started to read. Less than a minute passed before he looked up again.

"This isn't from Mrs Stanley. It's from a Pete Smith."

"I know," Fiona said. "It's a fake account she set up."

"Oh. Right." He pursed his lips. "And why on earth should I believe that? For all I know, you set up that email address yourself."

"Why would I do that? Why would I set up an email address to threaten my own mother?"

"I don't know? To try and get her off the hook?"

Fiona told herself to breathe and be calm—it was difficult. She glanced at Garda Fitzpatrick, as if appealing for some sense of reason. He jerked his head to one side. It was a subtle gesture, but the meaning was clear. He wasn't going to put his neck on the line.

"That's not true and I'll swear to it. It's Mrs Stanley. Look, Mam wasn't the only one she was blackmailing. I went to find the bucket beside the gate to Fleming's field and look what I found." She took the pin from her pocket, congratulating herself again on having the foresight to pick it up off the ground with a tissue, so as to preserve any fingerprints that were on it.

Sergeant Brennan leant across to look at the badge she'd dropped in the middle of the table. "What's this?"

"It's a badge. Somebody dropped it in the field near the drop-off point. It's a pin from the golf club. That should help narrow things down. And…" she sighed. She didn't know the legality of guessing somebody else's password, but there was no way she could explain the truth without referring to Granny Coyle's internet wizardry. "We found a Gmail address in the same name. We weren't able to get into the Facebook, but the Gmail address had the same password as Mrs Stanley's own Gmail address."

The sergeant's expression darkened. "And how, Miss McCabe, would you know *what* her password was?"

"We…I…I guessed it. It wasn't hard. She'd been using the computers at the library and her email address must have been saved in the cache there. I tried a few things and then thought of Fort Lauderdale. It's where her sister lives and apparently she was always mad to go there. There was nothing in her own Gmail but then we… I hit backspace to get out of Gmail and there it was. It was a little list of email addresses that had been accessed from that computer, and this name, Pete Smith, was on there. When I didn't recognise it, I had my suspicions and sure enough it opened with the same password as Mrs Stanley's email account."

He stared her in the eyes without saying anything, before turning to Garda Fitzpatrick. "What do you think, Garda?"

Fitzpatrick shook his head. "I don't know. I've never heard of anything like this around town."

"No, indeed. It seems far-fetched in the extreme. Tell me this: ye haven't been watching crime movies, have ye? That's the only explanation I can think of."

Fiona shook her head, unable to believe what she was hearing. "Crime movies? A woman is dead and my mother's after receiving a blackmail threat. Now, it's clear from Mrs Stanley's email address that she's been threatening more people. In fact, if you get on there, you'll see responses from a lot of people around Ballycashel. Now, is that not enough for you to get a warrant to get access to the Facebook profile? It's clear that one of those people is behind her murder. And these are people you didn't even suspect before.

"Bernard Boyle, for example. He's the secretary of the golf club and there was a message in there from him. You see? Maybe the golf club pin and the weird messages don't mean much alone, but together? There's something going on here."

Brennan blanched. He stared at her for a few moments, seemingly in disbelief. "It's a lovely little story." The corners of his mouth were working up and down, as if he was struggling to contain his anger.

"It's not," she said, working hard to stay calm. "It's a horrible story of greed and murder. I'm trying to help solve it."

"Why?" he jeered. "Do you not have enough on your hands running a failing pub? Maybe you should concentrate your energies on doing that instead of wasting Garda time and resources."

"I'm not wasting your time! I'm trying to give you important information!"

"Important information!" he cried, throwing the printed sheets back at her as if they were infected. "This proves nothing! I've never heard of Pete Smith. Why would she create a false name?"

"Um, to keep her identity hidden?"

"This is nonsense. You've no proof of that."

"Well look at the messages! Isn't it clear that there's a malicious intent behind them?"

He rolled his eyes so dramatically that he looked like a TV medium at a séance. "Would you go away with your malicious intent! How do I know these are even real? You could have put them together in Photoshop in some misguided attempt to get your mother off the hook!"

"I can barely even format a table in excel, never mind use Photoshop. Anyway, that's easily proven. We can log into Mammy's Facebook account now and I'll show you the messages."

"That won't be necessary."

"Don't you want to solve this thing?"

He shook his head. "As far as I'm concerned, you're wasting my time. You're trying to lay the blame at the feet of other Ballycashel citizens and you're mad if you think I'm going to tolerate that."

"It's real!" Fiona cried, jumping to her feet and slamming her fist on the table. "I can prove it to you if you'd only listen to me! What's the harm in investigating these people? I can give you the list."

"This isn't East Germany. You can't go around spying on your neighbours and getting them into trouble."

"I know it's not! And I'm not spying on anyone."

"You admitted yourself that you broke into Mrs Stanley's email account. Who knows what else you've been doing. I ought to charge you for that."

"Maybe you ought to," she cried, shaking her head and turning to leave. "Because it seems like you won't rest until you have a full collection of McCabes crowded into those cells back there!"

She stormed out, not waiting to hear his reply.

Garda Conway was at the desk. He smiled and nodded at her as she passed. "Howaya Fiona?"

"Hey, Garda Conway. Not great to tell you the truth. How do you put up with him? I don't understand it. I have leads in the case and he won't even listen."

Conway shook his head, glancing behind him with a hunted expression in his eyes. Fiona had seen the same look in her brother Enda's eyes after he'd been caught drinking on the night of the leaving cert results, and she knew there was something behind it.

"What?"

At that moment, Garda Fitzpatrick, Sergeant Brennan and Margaret McCabe emerged from the sergeant's office and Garda Conway went to great lengths to look away from Fiona. She stared at him, willing her to explain what had been going through his head, because it had seemed like he was just on the verge of telling her something important. But no, it looked as if he was busying himself with paperwork. She stood staring at him for a while before the sergeant's presence became repulsive.

"Come on, Mam. I've a good mind to make a complaint to the Garda Commissioner, only I know there's no point since he's firmly entrenched in the sergeant's father's best friend gang."

She stormed out without giving him a chance to reply. She felt no satisfaction at having delivered such an insult, only frustration at his obvious refusal to listen to what she'd been trying to tell him.

"Well, we tried," Margaret said after she'd delivered so much food to the sturdy kitchen table that the poor thing seemed to groan under its weight.

"Leave it to the guards," Kate muttered. "Don't let Fiona carry you away on one of her crusades."

"Is it so wrong that I want to keep Mammy out of jail?"

"She hasn't done anything wrong. They can't send her to jail."

"You're so naive!"

Francis dropped his knife and fork with a clatter. "Stop fighting. It'll do no-one any good."

"Fi has a point, Dad. We've got to do something." Marty looked around at them all.

Normally, she'd be heartened by the support, but she had lost all sense of optimism. She shook her head, feeling sickened by what she was about to say. "We've tried. We've tried everything. We can't get into that Facebook account and there's no point in incriminating myself with the Gardaí by shouting from the rooftops about it. It's obvious that Brennan isn't going to pay any heed to anything we've told him."

"Well what have we got? We've already found out a lot."

Fiona dropped her fork onto her plate. Her mother's roasts were usually something she looked forward to all day, but she found her appetite was diminished since their visit to the station. She just couldn't see a way forward in the face of the sergeant's refusal to listen.

"There's no point. If we can't get the Gardaí's support, we're not going to be able to put that information to use."

"Oh come on, Fi," Marty said with his usual good spirits. "Humour me. What's the harm in going through the details one more time?"

She sighed and pushed her plate away. She wasn't hungry anyway so what was the harm?

"Fine. We know that Alan Power somehow unmasked his blackmailer as Mrs Stanley. He's been in her house before and he broke in to steal her computer. He may or may not have paid her off.

"That could be the reason that she started to work from the library—maybe she got rattled that she could be tracked. Then again, maybe he waited at the gate or other drop-off point and found her out that way. Either way, I don't think he's our killer. If he was, it would have made far more sense for him to take the computer when he poisoned her, instead of going back for it. Plus there's the matter of timing. We know he couldn't have been in Ballycashel at the time she was poisoned.

"We know at least one of her other blackmail victims found out her identity, but we don't know who. We also found the golf club pin at the scene of the drop-off. Now, we haven't been able to pursue that because the secretary of the golf club happens to be on the list of blackmail victims slash suspects."

"That's not a problem," Francis said. "Leave it with me. I'll talk to Donnie and find out what's going on. Do you still have the pin?"

"No!" Margaret cried. "Fiona gave it to Brennan!"

Fi smiled and reached in her pocket. "Actually, Mam, I took it back. Remember when I slammed my hand on the table? I grabbed it when he was scowling at me. It's here. Of course, my fingerprints are probably all over it, but when they're not going to use it as evidence anyway…"

"Good woman, Fiona!"

Kate arched an immaculately plucked eyebrow. "For stealing evidence from a Garda station?"

"For working hard to keep Mam out of prison," Marty said harshly. "And if you've got nothing constructive to say, maybe you should go elsewhere."

Kate looked to her parents for support, but Francis simply shook his head. "Your brother makes a good point, Catherine."

At this, Kate jumped up and flounced away.

"Right," Francis said without flinching. "I'll speak to Donnie and show him the pin."

"Are you sure? What if he's close to the suspect? They're on the committee together."

"It might not necessarily be our suspect. In any case, Donnie is a good man; as straight-up as they come. I doubt he'll be unduly influenced."

The door opened and Kate entered the room.

"Ah, you've seen the error of your ways already."

"No," she muttered. "I just thought you should know that Garda Conway is at the door. I heard knocking when I passed—ye mustn't have noticed with all the commotion going on in here. He's here to see you, Fiona."

Fiona jumped to her feet and hurried out to the

hallway without another word. She found Garda Conway standing just inside the front door, shuffling awkwardly from foot-to-foot.

This is it, she thought.

It had to be. She had known there was something strange about his behaviour at the station earlier. She could think of no other reason for him to visit— they'd never been particularly friendly.

"Garda Conway," she said, trying to calm her racing mind and pay attention to everything about him.

"Fiona," he said with a nod.

"Is everything alright? I've never known you to call before."

He cleared his throat and stared at the ceiling.

For a while, she thought he wasn't going to utter another word. She stood watching him, anticipation growing within her with every passing second.

"Garda Conway?" she whispered.

She told herself to stop; to hold off and not get overexcited. After all, he might just have been selling tickets to a raffle for the GAA club, of which his two boys were members.

But there was definitely something off about his demeanour. He was a shy man, but she had never seen him like this. And then a thought struck her. It went beyond shyness. He seemed almost rattled by something.

"Can I get you a cup of tea or anything?" she asked, goosebumps starting to prickle the skin on her arms.

"No thanks, Fiona," he said, still not looking her in the eyes. "I can't stay long. Look, I'm sorry to bother you at home, but there's something important you should know. And I shouldn't even be telling you this."

25

"Is there somewhere we can talk?"

Fiona nodded. "We can chat here."

Something about his expression made her reconsider. She glanced behind her at the closed door to the kitchen, knowing there were probably several ears pressed against it. "Come on in here," she said, leading the way to her father's study.

"So," she said when she'd closed the door behind them.

"So," he repeated.

"Garda Conway, you look like there's something weighing heavily on you. I got the same feeling earlier in the station. I've tried but I can't think how this relates to me. What's going on?"

He sighed and sat down heavily in Francis McCabe's high-backed chair. Fiona sat opposite him on another armchair, her heart hammering in her chest.

She didn't know Garda Conway well, but she'd certainly known him for a very long time. And in that time, she'd never seen him rattled by anything. He had always seemed like your stereotypical Garda: strong, honest, reliable. He didn't seem like any of those things at that moment.

"Garda Conway? What is it? You're starting to worry me."

He looked up with haunted eyes. "You have to appreciate, Fiona, that I shouldn't even be here in the first place. I've only a year or two until retirement. God knows I should be keeping my head down and doing whatever that little eejit tells me."

She blanched. "Sergeant Brennan? I've never heard you say a bad word about him before."

"Yeah, well," he spat. "He's my boss, isn't he? I'm hardly going to go tearing strips out of him to anyone who'll listen. I'm not that much of a fool." He sat forward, resting his elbows on his knees and rubbing his face with huge, red hands. "Listen."

Fiona nodded. She'd been waiting for him to speak for a while now. She didn't want to risk saying anything in case she distracted him from whatever was on his mind. She had so many questions she wanted to ask: what was going on and why had he come to tell *her*? They were screaming around in her head, getting louder and louder the more she ignored them.

"Look, I thought I better come and tell you. It's obvious you've been doing a bit of digging on this case."

She nodded. "It's only natural: you lot suspect my mother."

"Oh of course." He nodded curtly. "Indeed it is."

"So you're here to tell me something about the case?"

He sighed heavily. "I believe so. You see, I'd never worked a murder case in my life before the one a few months back. Poor young Hanlon, it was an awful fate to befall a young fella. I'd always been stationed in small country towns much like this. And I know you young guns might think that's awful dull, but I liked it. They were simpler times. And I'd much rather deal with some missing kitten or a dispute over a card game than murders and assaults. Ah, we've had our fair share of assaults, especially after losing the county championship, but I'm not talking about the usual drunken messing."

She smiled and nodded that she understood, hoping it would encourage him to continue.

"So that last case was a first for me in many ways. Brennan's different of course. With his connections, of course he's been at the coalface of probably a dozen interesting, career-making cases. I've heard from a lad that used to work with him in Dublin that he was often allowed in to interview a suspect they believed was on the brink of confessing so he'd get his name down as the arresting officer. Had it handed to him on a plate, see."

Fiona nodded. She'd heard similar and had formed more or less the same opinion herself.

"Now, that's what I have trouble with at the moment. I can't tell whether it's down to incompetence or to arrogance."

"What is?" Fiona couldn't resist asking.

A shadow flickered across his face. She knew it must be hard for him.

"Garda Conway, I promise I won't repeat a word of what you tell me," she said gently. "I swear it."

He smiled. "And I believe you too. I don't know why he has it in for you. You're all good sorts, you McCabes."

"Thanks," she said, hoping he hadn't just lost his train of thought. "That's why it's so strange that he's fixated on my mother like this. Sure, she had that argument with Mrs Stanley in the middle of the street —I'll be the first to admit that that wasn't like her. But she wasn't at Mrs Stanley's house that day and she certainly didn't poison the woman. It's weird that the sergeant won't believe what we told him about the blackmail."

"What's that now?"

She remembered that Garda Conway hadn't been present when she and her mother had presented the evidence to the sergeant. She told him, pausing and doubling back several times in order to make sure she didn't leave any part of it out.

"It doesn't surprise me in the slightest."

"That's what I don't get," she whispered. "I mean, sure it sounds odd, but is it not worth checking out? Ye have technical people who could probably unravel the whole thing in a matter of hours." A thought struck her. "How about if I give you all the details? You could send it off behind his back."

He laughed, a sad sound that had no humour in it. "You're certainly your father's daughter alright. Francis McCabe always knew how to persuade those around him. It's why he made such a good coach. But I'm afraid I can't help you there. It's like I said: I have to put the years in until I reach pension age. After that I'm gone. I'm done watching these young bucks with connections waltzing in and taking over."

"Maybe he'll move on soon. He's bound to get promoted again soon because of his father."

"Oh, wouldn't we all love it! But we can't guarantee such a thing. Anyway, in a roundabout way that's kind of why I'm here. You see, I can't tell whether it's incompetence or something more sinister."

Fi gasped, her already overactive imagination going into overdrive. "Sinister?"

"You heard me. I know it's a very grave statement to make but that's the conclusion I'm being forced to draw." He shuffled around in the chair, working hard to make his bulky frame comfortable. Fiona thought for a moment that she should offer him some tea and biscuits again—or a glass of water at the very least—but she dismissed that thought. She was terrified to interrupt him lest he change his mind and disappear before he had a chance to tell her what had him so riled up.

"You're talking about the sergeant."

He jerked his head. "At first I barely noticed. It was little things. Like when we were examining the scene. We had to fight with him to fingerprint the place. Now, I'm no crime scene expert, but that seemed odd. He kept saying there was nothing to find. And now, don't even get me started on the evidence. I wanted to take away her computer—it seemed a very fancy one for a woman of her age and means. Brennan wouldn't hear of it. Told us there was no point what with it being smashed. Said she probably only used it for playing solitaire and looking up funeral times, and he didn't have time for business like that and I shouldn't either."

"Strange," she whispered. And before she even realised what she was saying, she continued. "I thought it was strange that the TV was still in there when…"

Fiona stopped and froze, her eyes widening as she realised the extent of her indiscretion.

But Garda Conway looked anything but shocked. In fact, his lips had twisted into a wide smile.

"You…"

"Ah, come on now. I wasn't born yesterday. Your father thought he was pulling a fast one by feeding me that information in the pub."

"You knew?" she gasped.

He shook his head, chuckling to himself. "I'm not an old fool."

"Why didn't you say anything? We could have gotten in serious trouble if you'd reported us."

"Why would I do that? Sure isn't it great when fellas want to do my job for me? The amount of information I've gotten that way down through the years… the bonus, of course, is getting to enjoy a few pints at the same time.

"Anyway, that was when things got very odd. I went to the house first thing to check it out; before I even told the sergeant what I'd learned. No-one from the force had been back there since the initial search the day before. It was obvious to me that her computer was gone, and it didn't seem like anything else had been touched. I was immediately suspicious. But I'm all for following protocol these days, so away I went into the station. I told the sergeant I'd heard two aul ones muttering about noises coming from Mrs Stanley's place late at night and that someone saw Alan Power loitering around.

"We set off to check. Brennan insisted on coming with me. We got in and the first thing I did was point out that the big fancy computer that had been there the day before wasn't there anymore. He heard me say it. Seemed to take it in. So away we went to pick up Power. But Brennan didn't even ask him about the computer. No, it was all about the murder. Now, I thought it might have been forgetfulness on his part so I scribbled a note on a piece of paper and passed it to him. And still he didn't mention it!"

"Why? Wasn't it relevant?"

"Well, Alan Power's alibis for the time of the murder checked out, but I would have thought

Brennan would be desperate to increase his arrest record. But he point blank ignored it. There was no search of Power's house even though it could have turned up something. In fact, Brennan just dropped the matter as soon as the building manager in Dublin sent us the proof to back up Power's alibi for the time of the murder."

"Did you mention it to him again?"

"Why would I bother? Like I said, I'm not interested in rocking the boat. I've put in my time."

"So, what's this about? You want me to rock the boat and find out what's going on?"

He stood to leave, walking as if his limbs were stiff. "I suppose I thought I owed it to you. Brennan seems keen to pin it on your mother and leave it at that, even in the face of evidence to suggest other parties are involved. Like I said, I can't decide if that's laziness or something else."

"You think…" she shook her head as she mulled over her words before she even dared to say them out loud. Brennan was obnoxious, sure, but was he capable of more than that? She had always thought he was a pain, but was he dangerous too? She took a deep breath and exhaled, knowing she was going to have to confront this head-on. "Do you think he's deliberately suppressing evidence? That he's in league with the murderer?"

Conway smiled and for a moment Fiona thought he was messing with her. But there was only sadness in his eyes. "I don't know what to think anymore, Fiona love. All I'll say is this: mind yourself. And if it ever looks like there's more to it than meets the eyes; or if you ever feel like you're in danger, you call me. That should be the first thing you do. Here," he said, taking out his phone. "I'll give you my number. I can't go throwing mud at the sergeant when I don't know if it's just my imagination. That doesn't mean I'd cast you into danger. Do you hear?"

She nodded. "If I find out anything, I'll call and let you know."

"Do that. I mean it. My hands are tied in terms of getting involved, but if there's something sinister going on then you let me know. I don't want you running off and breaking into crime scenes without Garda protection."

"I won't," she said laughing. "At least, I'll call you and let you know before I do. I promise."

"And you won't repeat a word of what I told you?"

She shook her head. "I won't."

"Of course you can tell your family. Lord knows I know your grandmother has been involved in the case with you as well. But outside of family, keep it to yourself, eh?"

"I will," she whispered, wondering if she'd even dare to make such accusations in public. If what Garda Conway was saying was true—and hadn't she seen the evidence of it herself—then it was possible they had a corrupt Garda sergeant on their hands.

The case had just gotten a whole lot more complicated.

THERE WASN'T a sound in the room as Fiona filled her family in on what Garda Conway had just told her. Even when she'd finished, none of them seemed capable of responding.

"Well?" she muttered, after what seemed like five minutes of pure silence.

Marty shook his head. "Unbelievable. Do you think Conway has gone mad?"

"No," she said, thinking back. "He was definitely acting strangely, but he was completely lucid. You know, he told me about Dad feeding him the story of Alan Power in the pub. Things like that. I don't think he's making it up, if that's what you mean. After all, haven't we seen these things ourselves with our own eyes? What do you think, Dad? You've known Garda Conway longer than any of us."

"I'm as surprised as the rest of you," Francis said. "He's always played the fool and played it well. I'm certainly not the first person to feed him information thinking he'd have a hazy memory of the source."

"So he's got a better memory than he lets on," Granny Coyle snapped. "So what? Is he expecting you to go and do his job for him?"

"I don't know," Fiona said with a sigh. "It seemed like he was telling me out of courtesy. It's not that he doesn't want to be involved, it's that he'll only get involved if he's certain there's foul play going on."

"Big of him."

"Ah Mammy," Margaret said. "He's a good man. Don't be too hard on him. He was certainly decent to me when they had me in for questioning."

They all fell silent. Fiona looked around at them, hoping at least someone would have an idea. No-one said anything.

"I think we should pay Alan Power a visit," Granny Coyle announced after several minutes.

Fiona blinked, wondering if she'd heard that correctly. "Excuse me?"

"You heard. Alan Power. We'll get him to tell us why he took that computer. That'll give us more to go on. Maybe he's even gotten onto her Facebook page."

"Just like that. You think he's just going to talk to us about breaking into her house?"

Granny Coyle shrugged. "I don't see what other options we've got."

"But you didn't listen to what I said earlier; what Conway told me. There's a possibility that Brennan is in cahoots with the murderer."

"There is of course, but I doubt it."

"You doubt it enough to go over there and reveal our hand to him?"

"Oh come on, Fiona. Don't be so cautious. What's the worst that can happen? Even if he is in cahoots with Brennan, we're not going to reveal anything to him that you and your mother haven't already told the guards. A few of us will go just to be on the safe side."

"And if he doesn't want to talk to us?"

Granny Coyle smiled but none of them were fooled. There was pure steel behind the pleasantry. "We'll make him talk to us. Don't worry."

Fiona looked around at the others as if beseeching them to talk some sense into her granny. It wasn't that she didn't have faith in Rose, she just wondered if she was persuasive enough to force a man to talk when he was at risk of incriminating himself.

"Come on, Fiona," Granny Coyle needled. "You said yourself that we don't have any options. I, for one, think we should have spoken with him before now."

"But he's not going to talk to us. You must know that. Remember what you said when you tried to draw him on whether he'd helped Mrs Stanley? You said he seemed like a nasty fella. He was dismissive. There's also the fact that he's been in her house. He may not have murdered her, but that doesn't mean other sinister things haven't gone on…" she shivered, remembering what Garda Conway had said about the sergeant. "And there is the possibility that he's connected with Brennan. What do you think of that? Incompetent or corrupt?"

They all shook their heads.

"Incompetent," Marty said.

"Both." Margaret pursed her lips and winced. "He treated me like a common criminal when it should have been obvious I had nothing to do with it."

"He's certainly incompetent," Granny Coyle said.

"Lookit," Francis drawled. "What does it matter? We'll find out one way or the other later. There's no point in dwelling on it."

"So your vote is to go speak to Alan Power then, Francis?"

"It is, Rose. Conway wouldn't have come here if he wasn't convinced that the only way for us to clear Margaret's name is to investigate this thing ourselves. And I can't see any other way of getting to the truth, can you? Now, I'll chat to Donnie tomorrow, but I think the first thing we should do is pay a little visit to Alan Power."

"Who do you mean we?" Ben asked, glancing longingly at the door to the sitting room that led off the kitchen.

"I mean we as in all of us," Francis said, glaring at his youngest son. "That means you too, Ben. I'm sure you can tear yourself away from that stupid console for an hour or two."

"But I was going to have a tournament with Barry," he moaned, before glancing around the table and seeing the disapproving faces that were watching him. "Of course," he muttered. "I'll go up and get my jacket."

Fiona still wasn't convinced about the plan. "Now? We're all just going to march over there now and confront him?"

Francis nodded. "Sure why not? He won't be expecting us and isn't there strength in numbers? Anyway, there's no sense in waiting until tomorrow because he'll be gone off to work in Dublin for the day. There's no time like the present."

FIONA CONSIDERED it a minor win that she'd convinced them to leave the hurleys at home. It hadn't been easy: Marty and her father had been all for bringing them along just in case trouble broke out. She had had to spell it out for them several times that trouble was likely to break out if they marched across town with hurleys in hand. Finally, she'd persuaded them based on the last time they'd gone out as a family with their sticks: some busybody had called the guards and they'd had to convince a sceptical Sergeant Brennan that they were going training, not to take the legs off someone.

"You're right, Fi," Marty said again. "Best not drawn Brennan's attention before we know what's going on with him."

"Though it does mean we're leaving ourselves defenceless," Francis said morosely. "That could be foolish."

"Dad, there's six of us. Eight if Colm and Enda get my message and join us. There's only one of him. And he's not exactly a highly-trained assassin. He works in IT for God's sake. The only things he's ever smashed are milestones and goalposts in a Gant chart."

"And the window to Mrs Stanley's house," her father added reasonably. "We're not sure yet what we're dealing with."

"Okay, okay," she said, holding up her hands and feeling foolish for being naïve. "Look, I'll call Colm. I'll ask him and Enda to wait a little bit down the road in the car. We'll work out a signal so they can come and back us up if we need it."

"Back us up!" Margaret exclaimed. "It sounds so glamorous, like something out of a movie."

"Yeah, it's not really," Fiona muttered. "I still think you should stay home, Mam. We don't want to be giving Brennan even more ammunition to use against you, do we?"

Her mother folded her arms. "I'm coming with you. I'm stuck in the middle of this thing and there's no way I'm hearing about it second-hand from the rest of you."

"Great, Ma," Ben said with a smirk. "You can play good cop to Granny's bad cop. Make him a nice cup of tea if he cooperates."

"Come on so," Fiona said, clapping her hands and pointing towards the door. She sensed an argument brewing and thought it best to get out of the house before it kicked off again.

———

"I'm NOT sure this is such a great idea," Margaret McCabe muttered in a stage whisper as they opened the gate of Power's terraced house and made their way onto his property one-by-one.

"Sure you were mad to join us earlier. What changed?"

"I don't know. I suppose I thought it'd be more glamorous."

Fiona shook her head. "Well you can't back out now. We don't want you wandering around on your own while we're all in there."

"I'm not a sheep," Margaret countered. "I'm well able to go around town on my own."

"You're supposed to be keeping a low profile, love," Granny Coyle said patiently.

"And I am! I've barely been out of the house all week."

"That's because the last time you ventured out you got into a public screaming match with a woman who ended up dead. What? I'm just saying it how it is, there's no need to look at me like that."

"It does sound pretty harsh, Granny," Marty said reasonably.

Francis, who was at the head of their little column, turned and made an exaggerated shushing sound. "Will you all please keep it down? We're here."

It was half seven at night, but because it was September, it was still bright outside. That gave them a disadvantage: at least if it had been dark they'd have been able to tell if anyone was home or not by whether the lights were on in the house.

Francis cleared his throat and rang the doorbell.

And then they waited.

"What if he's in but he doesn't answer the door?" Ben whispered.

Granny baulked. "And who in their right mind would answer the door to six people all frothing at the mouth for answers?"

"Good point," Fiona whispered, flattening herself against the wall of the porch.

The others followed suit, leaving Francis standing in the middle of the porch facing the peephole as if he'd come along by himself.

That was another thing, Fiona thought, frowning at the door. It was rare to see peepholes in the doors of houses like this, which must have been built in the fifties or sixties. Fair enough, it was common in new developments or houses that had been renovated, but it was clear this place hadn't even been painted in a long time, let alone renovated. Had Alan Power had it installed? Why would he need such a privacy measure in a place like Ballycashel?

Fiona swallowed. As the seconds passed, it seemed less and less likely that he was going to open the door. "Buzz again, Dad," she whispered as quietly as she could.

Francis did.

They waited for longer. Fiona held her breath and leant her head against the door, trying to hear any noise from inside the house. It seemed silent—there wasn't even the faint buzz from the TV.

"It doesn't look like he's here," Francis said at last. "Or if he is, he's not coming to the door."

The disappointment was visible on all of their faces. Fiona didn't realise it, but she'd been convinced this was going to be the end of the whole mad affair. Now it looked like they were going to have to wait even longer to find out what was going on.

"Come on so," she said, disheartened. "I suppose we should go."

The door remained unopened and they had no choice but to turn around and march back up the path. They had only gotten a few paces when an agitated-looking figure in Lycra appeared at the gate. Fiona watched without passing much heed for a few moments, until it became clear that he was opening the gate and marching down the path towards them.

"I've told you people before. I'm not interested in finding out the word of God."

"Nor am I, son," Francis said.

Alan Power stood there blinking. "What are you doing here then? What are you selling?"

"The cheek of him," Margaret whispered. "Do we look like a travelling band of salespeople?"

"We're not selling anything, young man. We need to speak to you."

Alan Power threw his hand up to his brow and groaned as if he was in agony. "I've just had the day from hell and now this? Look, whatever you're selling I'm not interested, okay? Move on to the next house."

Francis tutted. "My mother-in-law just told you. We're not here to sell anything. We're your neighbours of sorts. We're the McCabes. We live in town."

This time, Power looked them over warily. "Oh, yeah? I suppose you do seem familiar. Well then what do you want? I have a conference call at eight with the New York office. I'm afraid if it's not important I'm going to have to—"

"We know you broke into Mrs Stanley's house and took her computer," Fiona blurted. "So I think it's in your interests to talk to us."

He stood there staring at her, his mouth open in astonishment. She half expected to make a run for it, so she stepped forward and off to the side as subtly as she could to block his path.

"It was you," Power muttered. "It was you lot who put the Gardaí onto me. What possible reason could you have for doing that? I don't even know ye except to see."

Fiona shook her head, wondering how they were going to get him to speak. It was clear that he had no intention of helping them. She was going to have to wing it, she realised. It wasn't like she'd ever had experience of dealing with a situation like this before.

"We saw you. And we have you on camera."

This time his eyes widened. "Is that so?"

She nodded. "Yeah."

He stared at her for a few moments before bursting into laughter. It was the most horrible sound Fiona had ever heard.

"Of course you don't. If you did, why the hell would the guards have let me go and not charged me with robbery? You're making that up."

"Do you really want to test me?"

"I'll take my chances," he sniffed, pushing past them towards the door.

Fiona looked desperately at the others. He had his key out now. In a moment he'd have locked himself inside and their opportunity would be lost, but she couldn't think of a way to make him talk to them.

Granny Coyle strode forward after him. "The camera footage isn't the only thing," she said her voice full of mirth. "There's other material too. You might have thought you got Mrs Stanley's laptop but you didn't know she'd started logging in to Facebook in the library, did you? Unfortunately for you, she left her account logged in."

Power froze.

"I understand your reluctance now," Granny Coyle said gently. "I imagine if this got out, your reputation would take quite the hammering."

He stared at her without saying anything. Butterflies danced around in Fiona's stomach as she watched him, wondering what he was going to do. Would he call their bluff? Sure, Granny knew her way around a computer but this guy worked in IT for a living. Wasn't it possible he'd already gotten into her emails and Facebook and scrubbed any reference to himself?

"You would have told the guards," he said. The hesitation in his voice was unmistakeable.

"Would we? Do you know Mrs Stanley was a good friend of mine and I've been wondering how she managed to afford that lovely new computer and TV of hers? Now that I know, why on earth would I go throwing my meal ticket away but telling the guards what I know?"

Alan Power seemed to crumple before them. "What do you mean, your meal ticket?"

Rose smiled. "We need to talk. Aren't you going to invite us in?"

Fiona felt a brief moment of sympathy for Alan Power. He had sat at the head of his slick glass and oak table, and was staring them down as if he meant business. His hands gave the game away. He had them clasped together on the table in front of him, but that wasn't enough to stop them from trembling.

She supposed it was a double whammy: the threat of his deepest darkest secrets getting out as well as the intimidation factor of six people clustered around his table and baying for blood.

But if it meant clearing her mother's name for good? Fiona was willing to get in on the act and do anything to get the truth out of him.

"What do you want? This is... this is so wrong. I

told Mrs Stanley that. At least she had the decency to try and hide her name."

"But you found it."

"I did." He sniffed. "It amazes me that she thought she could pull the wool over my eyes. I work in IT for God's sake."

"So you've said."

His eyes narrowed. "That's so typical of Ireland. Begrudgery left, right and centre. It's a statement of fact."

"There's no begrudgery here," Granny Coyle said matter-of-factly. "I was just pointing out that you've mentioned that a number of times already. We *know*." She leaned forward, fixing her with steely blue eyes. "Now, what we don't know is where you put that computer. Why'd you steal it, Mr Power? You must have known they wouldn't take it."

"Of course I didn't," he spluttered. "If anything, I went over there with the sinking feeling that it was sitting in a Garda lab somewhere."

"But it was broken."

"I didn't know that until I got there."

"Why'd you bother even going over if you think the Gardaí had it? Why didn't you just sit at home all tucked up on your fancy leather sofa and watch your giant flat-screen telly?"

Hurt darted through his eyes. "If that's not

begrudgery I don't know what is. I work hard for my money."

"I'm sure you do," Granny muttered. "Working hard on reports nobody'll ever read and getting paid six figures to do it. Meanwhile, nurses and teachers are fighting hard to make anything over a pittance. It's extraordinary really. It beggars belief. There used to be a time where important professions like that could rely on being well-paid and—"

"Granny," Fiona whispered knowing her grandmother could talk at length about that topic without coming up for air. "You can tell him what a so-and-so he is later. Isn't there something else you want to say?"

Rose rolled her eyes. "Excuse me for caring about the fabric of this country. Yes, there is as it happens."

"Oh for God's sake," Power groaned. "I told you I had a conference call at eight."

"There'll be no more conference calls for you if I tell your bosses what I know," Granny Coyle whispered, her eyes glinting dangerously.

"Just tell me what you want then! I already paid her off. That should have been an end to it."

Granny Coyle pretended to consider this, tapping at her chin and glancing up at the glittering light fitting above them.

"You want that? You can take it," Power said, following her gaze.

Granny Coyle looked back at him as if he was something that had arrived in the bottom of her shoe. "*That*? You think I want that? It's the ugliest thing I've ever seen in my life. And I've seen a lot of ugly things: I was around in the fifties when the equivalent of a six-pack was a hairy gut and a few yards of road frontage."

Power blinked at her uncomprehending. Fiona snorted and quickly turned away to disguise the laughter she simply couldn't hold back.

"I don't understand."

"Of course you don't," Granny sighed. "You lot never do. I'll spell it out for you so. You give me Mrs Stanley's computer and we'll consider the matter over. You'll never hear a word from us again."

"How can I get comfort that that's true? I need reassurances—"

"Look here, sunshine," Francis said with a scowl. "This isn't the time and place for your jargon. Your comfort is the least of our worries. Now. Granny Coyle here has your office's main line number on speed dial. Hand over that computer and let us get back to the comfort of our own home before I go mad."

Power closed his eyes and shook his head, solemn as a priest. "I'm afraid it's not that simple."

"It's pretty simple," Granny Coyle said. "Give us the computer or I'll have a nice chat to your boss."

"There are over two hundred employees at my firm," Power replied, regaining some of his former cockiness. "And you're telling me you know who I work for?"

She rolled her eyes. "Of course not. But I'm capable of asking for Alan Power's line manager now, am I not?"

"They'll never put you through. He's too important."

"Do you want to run that risk?"

They stared each other down for a few minute before Power threw his head back with an almighty sigh.

"I don't have it," he groaned. "I destroyed it the minute I got back here."

"Why would you take an already-broken computer just to destroy it?"

"Isn't it obvious? I couldn't risk leaving it out there. I had to see if the guards had taken it."

"Why'd you destroy it even more then?"

He pursed his lips. "I had to."

"I don't believe you," Granny Coyle said simply.

"Go ahead and search the place if you want," he

wailed. "I don't see why you want the damn thing anyway. It's not like she had any real dirt on you. And only an expert like me would have been capable of getting into the files anyway the way it was left."

He was looking straight at Margaret as he said this, but it took a while for them to realise the significance of this. When they did, there was an almost palpable effort from them not to show their reactions in case Power noted their surprise. Everyone stayed silent as if they'd agreed to let Granny Coyle do the talking.

"Well, who's to say," Granny Coyle said after a few minutes' pause. Her expression was as inscrutable as ever.

"Oh come on," Power scoffed. "Stiffing the church collection? Compared to some of the crimes that were on there? It's nothing."

"It is not nothing," Margaret cried suddenly, standing and hurrying to the window.

"Not for her."

Power rolled his eyes. "It's ridiculous."

"I'd advise you not to say such things about my daughter in my presence," Granny Coyle said. "Or have you forgotten who has all the bargaining power here?"

Power pursed his lips together so tightly they

started to turn pale. It was as if he didn't trust himself to speak.

"Well?"

He shook his head.

"I didn't hear you, Power."

Fiona smiled to herself. She would have felt sorry for the guy if he didn't seem like a complete pain. Her granny's interrogation techniques had always been intimidating whenever she'd suspected them of doing anything wrong as children. It was a relief to be on the other side of the table now.

"I'm well aware," he muttered.

"Great," Granny Coyle said airily. "We'll agree to differ on the seriousness or otherwise of leaving the collection envelope short. I don't think we'll ever come to an agreement; not even within the family." She shot him a smile. It was almost possible to believe there was real warmth behind it. "Anyway. It's clear you had a good look before you destroyed the drive."

He clicked his tongue. "Well of course. After I managed to get in there I had to see what dirt she had on others, didn't I?"

"You destroyed evidence."

"I don't know why you're getting so high and mighty. The only reason you're here is because you saw what she had on me."

Granny shook her head. "What did you see on there?"

"I hardly think… it's not…" he blustered.

"Well, speak up. There's not long until your conference call and I'd hate for you to miss it. What did you see? And how did you destroy it?"

"Not that it'll mean anything to you, but I held a strong magnet to it, soaked it in bleach and then salt water before burning the whole thing."

That reminded Fi of something. "Where'd you burn it?"

He smirked. "Where do you think? I went to the Garda station and did it there. I put it in the range cooker, of course. And an awful stink it made too."

Fiona frowned. Of course, she realised, the timing was all off. She had walked into that plume of smoke outside the Mahony's before Alan Power had even broken into Mrs Stanley's. It hadn't struck her as odd at the time so much as irritating, but now it stuck in her mind.

Trish Mahony was one of the people on Mrs Stanley's list. What had she been burning on the day of the murder?

Frustratingly, now wasn't the time to reflect on such things.

"So it's destroyed beyond repair," Fiona summarised.

"Yes," Power said, looking at her as if she was an idiot.

"So much for mounting the drive and retrieving the data," Marty muttered.

Power glared at him. "Ah, so we've a computer expert in our midst, do we? Ah sure that's great. Maybe you can sit in on my call, teach us all a thing or two."

Fi rolled her eyes. "I have to say, you're not making this any easier for yourself. Did no one tell you sarcasm is the lowest form of wit?"

"Will you just get on with it!" he shouted suddenly, face becoming a worrying reddish-purple. "I've had about all I can take of you people and your incessant talking. It's enough to drive a man mad."

"Answer my questions and we'll leave you be."

"Your questions? I thought you just wanted the computer."

"I did," Granny Coyle said, shaking her head and smiling sadly. "But you just told me you destroyed it. So this is the alternative."

"Fine," Powers said, sighing and sinking back into his chair as if doing so allowed him to pretend they weren't there.

"First things first. Why did the Gardaí let you go?"

"What? Why?" he started to bluster but

something about her expression must have made him think twice about doing so. "Because I didn't do anything wrong. I was in Dublin at the time she was poisoned. My company forwarded the Gardaí the CCTV footage to prove it."

"Aha. But you left in the afternoon and never went back."

He flushed. "I had a meeting offsite."

"There was the break-in too. Why didn't they arrest you for that?"

He shrugged. "They never asked me about that. Come to think of it, nobody knows about it except for you." He leant forward, staring into her face. "How exactly do you know about that?"

Rose shook her head. "I'm not here to answer questions. Now, clarify that like a good lad. They didn't mention the break-in to you at all?"

"No. That's what I said. Is that it?"

"Oh no, son," Granny Coyle said, shaking her head and chuckling. "Not at all. We'll be here a while yet. But you're doing great." She leaned over and patted his hand before he abruptly pulled it away as if she'd injured him. "Now. When did you first meet Mrs Stanley? And when did you first visit her house?"

He coloured. "I've never been in her house. At

least, I'd never been there since… since the other day." He looked unsure of himself for the first time.

"We know that's not true."

"It's the truth. It's… I… Oh, fine. If you must know, I paid her a visit some time back. She'd emailed me, you see. Using a fake name on Facebook. At first I thought it was a joke, but I kept on getting messages and they started to threaten my job." His expression hardened. "I won't tolerate a threat to my livelihood."

"You're very intimidating," Granny Coyle said cheerfully. "Carry on there. The clock is ticking and I'd hate for you to miss your call."

He turned puce again, but this time he said nothing.

"You were telling us about your first visit over there."

"Yes," he said, the 's' sound coming out as a hiss. It seemed appropriate: there was something inherently snake-like about him. "It was easy. She'd done nothing to hide her IP address. I was able to trace it back to her once I grew concerned that this Pete Smith wasn't going to let it go."

"I see. So you went to threaten her."

He rolled his eyes. "I went to tell her I knew what was going on. I didn't even know who I was visiting until I knocked on the door and this seemingly-sweet old lady opened it. That's until a few seconds passed and I saw the fear in her eyes when she saw it was me."

"So you intimidated her."

"No," he groaned. "She made it clear to me that she had something on me and she wasn't going to keep quiet about it unless I paid up."

"So what did you do?"

He shook his head. "If this gets out, I could get in serious trouble over it."

"More serious than the trouble you're already in?"

"Fine!" Power shouted. "I left, making out like I was some chastened little schoolboy who she'd outsmarted. I went home and set about finding a Trojan horse that I could use to get in and wipe her hard drive. I stayed up all night doing it too."

"Quite the boy scout."

"She tried to blackmail me!"

"Fair enough," Fiona said, getting the feeling there were too many bad cops in the room and not enough good cops. "I'd do the same if someone tried to blackmail me."

"Oh, I feel so consoled by that," Power sneered.

Okay, Fiona thought. *Back to bad cop if that's what you're going to be like.* She sat back in her chair and stared at him, wishing they didn't need him. But they did.

"So you sent her a virus. What then? Why kill her?"

"I didn't kill her."

"So you said. Why steal her computer?"

He slammed both hands on the table, startling them. He'd been sitting relatively still until that point. "Because she didn't open them! Two emails a day I sent her. I devised all sorts of clever emails to induce her to open them. I advertised cleaning products and bingo holidays. No matter what I did, they went unopened."

"They obviously weren't as clever as you thought," Granny Coyle snapped.

"No," he said sullenly.

"So you killed her," Ben prompted, a big grin on his face.

"No, you moron," Power snapped. "Did you not hear what I just said? I went back over there to talk some sense into her."

"To take her computer, you mean."

He scowled. "Whatever it took."

"And when was this? I take it the emails from her had stopped by then."

"They had, but the threat remained. Every time I saw her in town she'd look at me with those beady little eyes and I'd know she was just biding her time before she went to my boss and told him everything."

"So you killed her," Fiona prompted, suspecting he was very close to being tipped over the edge.

"I didn't kill her!" he screamed, leaping to his feet. "What is wrong with you people? I couldn't stand it anymore so I went over there with the intention of taking her computer when she was out, but when I got round to the back of the house the plan changed."

"What was that?" Granny asked, her face twisted into a look of disbelief.

"Because," he spat. "I could see her through the net curtain on the back door."

"So you didn't knock on the door and try to twist her arm."

"No. I didn't. Because I could see she was lying face down in her breakfast plate."

Fiona's heart started to pound. "When was this, Alan?"

"Just before they found her," he said as if it was obvious.

"But I don't get it," Francis said, shaking his head. "Why didn't you go in? You could have broken the lock and took the computer, then told the guards you were going in to help her."

Power shot him a look of pure disdain. "Do you think I'm an absolute fool? Of course I'd have done that. It would have saved me a lot of trouble."

"Why didn't you, then?"

"Because," Power snapped, looking fit to murder the whole lot of them. "Because there was somebody else there and I knew better than to storm in when it was clear they had something to do with it."

29

THE SILENCE in the room was deafening.

Fiona's throat had suddenly become dryer than she'd ever experienced. She looked around at the others, working hard to get her thoughts in order enough to form words, never mind meaningful sentences.

Granny Coyle seemed to recover fastest. "There was someone there you say? So what did you do?"

"I ran. Obviously."

"Did you call the guards?"

He pursed his lips. "I did not. I planned to wait an hour and then go back, but by then word had gotten out. Someone must have heard something."

"Wait," Fiona whispered, holding up her hand. "Who was there?"

She went through the list of suspects in her head. There were far too many to even think of narrowing them down without the help of the guards. She had never imagined they would find out the killer's identity from Power —it seemed so unlikely that there had been a witness to the crime who hadn't come forward.

"I'll let you guess," he said sniffily. "I'm sure you can do it based on the list of people she was blackmailing."

Fiona raced through those names in her head, but none jumped out at her. What if he called their bluff? Frantically, she tried to narrow down the suspects, but the only lead they had was that poison was a female weapon of choice—and where had they even heard that anyway? For all she knew, it was just some urban legend.

The only thing they knew for sure was that Power had been frightened enough by whatever—or whoever—he saw to run away and risk leaving that computer, with its incriminating information. Who could have scared him to such an extent?

Thankfully, Rose wasn't about to start guessing. "You're running out of time. Why don't you tell us?"

Power sighed. "How do I even know you've got anything on me? For all I know, you're just bluffing. After all, I know she was trying to blackmail you too.

You could have just put two and two together. One of you went for a drive past her house that night and happened to see me on the road. So what?"

"That's rubbish," Granny Coyle said, clicking her tongue. "Now tell us, before I run out of patience and call your manager."

But Power seemed to be standing firm now. There was a glint in his eye that Fiona didn't like one bit. They'd dragged it out too long, she knew. And now he was calling their bluff.

Before she knew what she was doing, inspiration struck. "Oh, please Mrs Stanley," she whimpered in a put-on voice she hoped sounded like Power's own. "You must reconsider. I'm working on a very important project for my company. You can imagine what my dismissal would do to that progress and the effect it would have on the wider economy."

Power blanched.

"Would you like me to go on? As I recall, you begged for at least four *long* paragraphs. It was pretty pathetic really."

"Fine," he whispered. "Fine. It was a woman."

"Go on."

"That's all I saw. She was rooting around in the presses like she was possessed."

Fiona looked at her grandmother and saw her own frustration mirrored back in Rose's eyes. "What do you mean, that's all you saw. You said you saw the murderer."

"I did," he whispered. His hands were trembling again. "Well, I saw a woman. I don't know who she was."

"An awful lot of help that is. Was she tall? Small? What colour hair did she have? How was she dressed?"

There were three women on the list aside from Margaret. Sure, that narrowed things down but it wasn't as specific as Fiona had hoped. She sighed.

"You were afraid of her. Why?" She could understand why someone might have been intimidated by Louise Graham or Trish Mahony; Mrs Roche less so. She was a sweet woman with a permanent smile on her face.

"Because Mrs Stanley was bent over with her head in a plate," he snapped. "And there was something about her—the killer. A strange sort of ruthlessness in her movements. She was pulling the place apart."

"How old was she?"

"Thirties. Forties. Fifties. I don't know."

"You can't narrow it down any more? I suppose it eliminates Mrs Roche. She's in her seventies."

"I have no idea. I just caught a fleeting glance. She kept shrugging her shoulder. Sort of like this." He made an exaggerated gesture, shrugging one shoulder while relaxing the other. "And it seemed like she was only using one hand. I don't know. Maybe she was carrying a weapon."

Fiona frowned. "That's all you've got?"

"It was weird. A strange movement."

"You noticed that before noticed her hair? Really?"

"I saw all this through a net curtain. There was a dead woman in the room. You'll excuse me if I didn't commit a carbon copy of the scene to my memory."

"That's all you remember?"

"Isn't that what I told you? Now, are we done? Have you got your pound of flesh from me yet?"

Granny sighed. "More like a pound of pure tripe."

"Hey," Power protested. "I've told you everything I saw."

"Alan," Fiona said, squeezing her temples. "Just one more question. What do you remember from the files on Mrs Stanley's computer; about the other blackmail victims?"

"What?" he sneered. "You want to make sure you didn't miss out on anyone?"

The thought sickened Fiona, but she knew better than to object. After all, wasn't that what they were pretending they were up to in order to get information out of him?

"Maybe we do. What's it to you? Do you want to sacrifice yourself for the sake of a few random people you don't know?"

He seemed to consider this for a moment before he turned his head away and stared out the window beyond them. "No, I suppose I don't. Why should I fall on my sword? I do it often enough at work. Let's see, I didn't memorise them."

"You should have."

"Well I didn't know you were going to barge your way in here, did I? I'm not sure I can remember all the names. There was a red haired woman I've seen around the town. Her file had no information in it, just pictures. Her and a gentleman in a suit. It looked like they were on a city street. Georgian buildings. Dublin maybe. Arm-in-arm."

Fiona shook her head. She might have doubted his word if she hadn't witnessed Trish Mahony's little bonfire on the day of the murder. She wondered if she should go round there and see if there was anything left, but she doubted it. What had Trish been burning?

"What else?"

"Another woman. Roche I think her name was. Hers was more a list of crimes, if you could call it that. Sending poison pen letters. That sort of thing. There was no evidence in there that I could see, only dates and recipients."

Rose gasped.

"I'm only telling you what I saw."

"I don't believe it."

"Then you," Power went on, looking straight at Margaret. "Though I didn't know who you were at the time when I saw the list, only for there was a picture in there. Not very flattering if I do say so."

"Nobody asked for your opinion," Margaret said testily.

"Calm down, Ma," Ben said. "It was a sneaky photo of you at the bar in Phelan's. Of course it wasn't flattering."

"Oh it was far more flattering than the pictures of Louise Graham," Power said, smiling for the first time since they had arrived. "Whatever possessed her to take her clothes off and get in front of the camera I'll never know."

"Wait a minute," Ben blurted. "Louise Graham as in the woman from the gym?"

They all turned to look at him.

"There's only one Louise Graham that I know in town. So yes."

"I was only asking. I know her. I've been to that gym a few times."

"If you'd seen these pictures at all," Power said suspiciously. "You wouldn't be asking if it was your woman from the gym. These were the kind of snaps you'd seen in a men's magazine."

"We didn't look at all the pictures in detail," Fiona whispered. "Out of respect for the poor people in them."

"Then you can't have—"

"Go on."

Powers coloured. "Nothing."

"Oh don't worry, love," Rose chimed in. "We looked at yours accidentally. Now *there's* an image I can't get out of my mind."

Fiona glared at her, hoping her grandmother hadn't gone too far. The sight of Power's face made her relieved. Granny Coyle had obviously hit close to the truth.

Fiona cleared her throat, thinking it best to keep the pressure on in case Power had time to grow suspicious again. "So that's all the women?"

He narrowed his eyes. "Yeah. So?"

Fiona and her grandmother exchanged glances.

"Could be an older version of the files," Granny Coyle muttered.

"That's true," Fiona said. "I wonder if it's the same for the men."

"Sure didn't I tell you it was a woman?"

"Humour us," Francis said, flashing him a smile that seemed full of warmth and friendliness.

"Fine. Alright," Power said. He looked exhausted by now and Fiona knew they wouldn't get much more out of him.

He started to list the men she'd seen messages from in Mrs Stanley's secret email account. There was one surprise addition: it turned out that Mrs Stanley had been trying to blackmail Gerry Reynolds for taking part in a robbery.

Francis rolled his eyes. "I bet she didn't get very far with that. If anything, he's the kind of lunatic who'd get off on having the town know about his crimes."

Power ignored him. He was speaking faster now, as if the faster he went, the sooner he'd be rid of them.

Fiona had stopped listening. She was thinking about what Power had said about the female suspects. That changed when she heard Bernard Boyle's name.

"There was a load of pictures of him. No name but I recognised him straight away. He's the secretary of the golf club. And oh my. Do you know, if I hadn't seen that woman there with my own eyes, I'd have put money on him being behind the murder. And I'm not a betting man, let me tell you. No, those pictures." His eyes narrowed. "But I'm sure you know all this. Do we really need to go to the trouble of—"

"Yes," Fiona snapped. "We do. It's important to know if there's anyone we missed."

"Really? You intend to blackmail Bernard Boyle? Really?"

"That's none of your concern."

Power leaned back, shaking his head. "Then I sincerely doubt that you saw the pictures I've seen. I don't know why I'm even telling you this. I should let you carry on."

"Maybe you should."

"Foolhardy. Well, I don't think you'd be so brave if you'd come across the picture of Boyle over in the golf course handing a nice little brown envelope to the Garda sergeant. Would you?"

This time, none of them could hide their surprise.

"A brown envelope?"

Power nodded, smug at catching them out on their ignorance. "Didn't see that one, did you?"

"Maybe not," Francis muttered, eyes locked on his mother-in-law's. "But that doesn't help you out here."

All of a sudden, Fiona couldn't take it anymore. She had learnt enough. They had narrowed down their list of suspects and it was now crystal clear why

Sergeant Brennan had chosen to ignore the matter of the stolen computer.

There was no sense in drawing it out any longer. They had all the information they needed. It was just a pity that she had no idea at all how to put it to good use.

"Come on," she said, standing up. "He's not going to tell us anything useful. Look at him. He's terrified. Come on. Let's go."

"So that's it?" Power, looking resentfully at Granny Coyle.

She nodded. "More or less."

"How do I know that for sure? I need confirmation."

Granny Coyle looked at Fiona, who could tell what she was thinking. While they could have put him out of his misery right there and then, it made little sense to do so when they might need him to cooperate down the line. If it was anybody else, Fiona might have felt guilty for causing him worry, but this was Alan Power. He was already up there with Robocop on her list of most-despised people in Ballycashel.

And that was something else too. She had always suspected Robocop had gotten where he was from his father's connections, but that was a whole different ballgame to out-and-out corruption. If Alan

Power was telling the truth, then Brennan was taking backhanders.

She shook her head. It was all too much to take in.

"We'll be in touch," she told Power, before turning and heading to the door.

30

"WHAT AN OBNOXIOUS LITTLE TWIT," Francis muttered as they let themselves out the gate and onto the footpath.

Fiona shrugged. He certainly got his comeuppance in there, that's for sure. I almost felt sorry for the guy."

"I didn't," Margaret sniffed. "He's very full of himself. Thinks he's God's gift."

Any further discussion ended when Colm and Enda rolled up in Marty's station wagon.

"How'd it go? I have to say, ye were in there so long I was worried. I almost called the guards."

The others looked at each other with very serious expressions. "It's lucky you didn't."

Colm started to laugh. "I was exaggerating,

obviously. Sure I knew you were blaggarding. Are you finished?"

Francis nodded curtly.

"Mam, Granny, do you need a lift?"

Margaret started to climb into the car but stopped when Granny Coyle shook her head.

"No thanks, lads. I think the walk will do us good. We've a lot to take in."

"HE NEVER COPPED that we knew nothing," Ben crowed, when they were a safe distance away from Power's house and were sure of not being overheard.

"He came close. And we still don't know what she had on him."

"You're both missing the point," Fiona said, shaking her head. "It doesn't matter what she had on him. It was obviously something damaging enough that he couldn't risk kicking us out of his house without telling us anything."

"You're right. I suppose we should be thankful."

"Hmm."

Nobody said much until they got home. As soon as they got in the door, Fiona started to feel restless again. It was as if there was something she wasn't seeing in all of this. The irritating thing was, no matter how hard she thought about it, she couldn't think of what it was.

"Come on, Fi," Marty said, slapping her shoulder. "I'll drop you home if you want. Mam says you did great in there."

She sighed. "I suppose. Did she tell you what we learnt about Brennan?"

He nodded. "She did and all. I'm surprised. I never liked him, but I always thought he was straight-laced at the back of it all. It's shocking— considering he's supposed to be upholding the law and not breaking it. Do you believe Alan Power?"

She shrugged. "That's the thing. We have no reason not to, I suppose. But he could be making it all up."

Even as she said it, a little voice insisted that he wasn't. Sadly, that little voice didn't seem very keen on shedding any light as to why.

Finally, she made herself stop thinking about it. She was bone-tired, and the rest of her family were the same. What was the sense in drawing things out any longer when they could just reconvene and talk about it in the morning when they were rested?

She followed Colm and Marty to the door after saying goodnight to the others.

FIONA WOKE WITH A JOLT. She sat up with a gasp as a strange uneasy feeling shot through her. At first that alarmed her, but she soon realised it was the aftereffect of the dream she'd been having.

In it, a faceless woman had been chasing her through the streets of Ballycashel, trying to force a full breakfast on her. Fiona shook her head. She couldn't for the life of her conjure up an image of the woman's face. It was as if she was one of those people from the old cartoons: always slightly obscured or disjointed in some way.

She rubbed her eyes and reached over to the bedside table to retrieve her phone. She didn't even bother wasting time writing down the details of the dream—it wasn't as if its meaning was in any way cryptic after the day they'd had.

Fiona groaned. It was only half past three in the morning and by now she felt wide awake. Not only that, but she was thirsty. The water bottle on the bedside table was almost empty, not that she felt like more water. She'd been all but mainlining it in an attempt to increase her intake to the recommended eight glasses a day.

She had a sudden hankering for a cup of tea, even though she'd been trying hard to back.

"I don't need it," she muttered, immediately

feeling like an addict for having to tell herself that. Out loud. In the middle of the night.

Her words had little effect. Before she knew it, she was throwing off the covers and padding out of the bedroom into her little combined kitchen-living room. She switched on the kettle, threw a teabag in a cup and pulled open the fridge.

"Oh for God's sake," she muttered.

There was so little milk left that the carton felt empty. She hadn't noticed earlier—if she had she would have nipped down to the pub and borrowed a carton from the fridge there.

She looked around, rubbing her arms against the night-time chill. There was only one thing for it.

Sighing, she threw on a pair of runners and pulled a hoodie over her head. She debated bringing a hurley, but told herself it was time to stop that nonsense.

She would never admit it to anyone, but the place creeped her out in the middle of the night when it was all dark and devoid of people. She couldn't explain it. It was like the ghosts of all those who used to drink there still sat on the stools, just beyond her realm of sight.

She supposed it was something to do with the building dating back two centuries. It had a history. And she couldn't imagine that a pub, of all places, would have an uneventful history. Troubled souls and all that.

She rolled her eyes as she reached the ground floor. "You've too active an imagination, that's your problem. It's a pity you can't put it to better use than getting scared about ghosts."

She felt a bit more resolve after she'd given herself that pep talk, but it still didn't stop her from pausing and making sure she'd switched on every single light in the place.

It was slightly less creepy when it was fully lit. Ah, it wasn't creepy at all, she knew, it was just her mind playing tricks on her. If any of her family knew about her little fear, they'd no doubt have great fun sneaking into the place at night and banging a floor brush against the floorboards to try and scare her.

That's why they'd never hear about it—not from her anyway.

She padded across the floor, focussing her mind on imagining the pub full of customers. She thought back to the previous week. It was funny—on their second and subsequent visits, people tended to gravitate to the same seats as they'd taken previously, even if the rest of the place was free. It was a funny trait she'd noticed.

The exception was Louise Graham, she thought. She was very hard to pin down. Sometimes she sat in the corner; other times she lingered at the bar chatting to anyone who'd listen to her stories about her weight-lifting.

Fiona froze, halfway between the door and the bar.

Weight-lifting.

Her heart started to race as she remembered the last conversation she'd overheard between Louise and her friend. The truth was she'd drowned most of it out. She'd never been very interested in people who tried to push their sport onto others, and that was something Louise tried to do everywhere she went. She'd even tried to get Margaret McCabe down to the gym to do a trial class. She'd given Fiona the hard sell once before Fi made it clear that she wouldn't be joining under any circumstances.

That hadn't stopped her talking incessantly about it in the pub.

Fi closed her eyes. What had they been saying? Then she remembered it.

Louise was giving out about one of her training partners. He'd done something wrong and as a result, Louise had twisted the wrong way as she dropped the bar awkwardly.

She'd then gone on to talk about the risk of injury saying it now looked like she'd have to stop exercising for a while until her muscle healed. She supposed it was good timing with her heading to teacher training college later in the month.

That was it! Fiona shook her head in disbelief at her own oversight. It was all so clear—why hadn't she thought of it? Mrs Stanley must have somehow— God only knew how—found out about the naked pictures and figured she was onto something when she learnt that Louise wanted to train to be a teacher. If those pictures were as sordid as Alan Power had implied, they could ruin her career before it even started.

Fiona had forgotten all about the tea. She turned and started to run back to the door, cursing herself for leaving her phone upstairs. She wasn't worried about the late hour—she knew that Granny Coyle would be mad at her if she *didn't* call immediately to tell her the news.

"She's not going to believe this," she muttered, only pausing to pull the door closed after her.

"No, I don't imagine so," said a cold voice from behind her.

Fiona gasped, momentarily stunned from the shock. At first she thought it was her mind playing tricks again, but no. Unfortunately the man standing behind her was very real. And so was the knife in his hand.

31

"WHAT ARE YOU DOING HERE?" she hissed when she had recovered her nerves enough to be able to speak.

As she said it, she backed away slowly, thinking if she was lucky and fast, she might be able to get up the stairs fast enough to slam the door behind her and lock it. There wasn't enough time to close the door right behind her—to do so, she'd need to reach across and pull it in. He'd have no trouble catching her before she managed to get the door locked.

Her heart contracted with fear. She was assuming she'd be able to beat him up the stairs—but what if he caught up with her before she locked the door? She looked around for an alternative. Her phone was upstairs and the landline was all the way behind the bar.

He must have caught her glancing at it.

"Stop moving," he barked. "And don't even think about going for the phone. I disconnected it."

"When?" she snapped, forgetting herself. "How long have you been in here?"

"Not long," he sneered. "I wasn't expecting you to come down here. You gave me quite a shock."

She shivered at the implication of what might have happened if she hadn't woken up; if there had been milk in the fridge and she'd just had her cup of tea and gone back to bed.

Then she steeled herself. She wasn't going to show any fear in front of this eejit, even if he had a knife in his hand. It looked like a good one too—it was just typical. Why couldn't he have the same cheap, half-blunt knives she had in her kitchen? That one looked not just expensive, but sharp. Still, despite the knife, Fiona appeared to have some sort of malfunctioning fight or flight response, where her body opted for the foolish third option: sarcasm.

"Sorry if I inconvenienced you, Alan. How rude of me."

He pursed his lips. "I see you've given up the facade of being nice. It doesn't matter to me. I don't care if you beg, it's not going to have any effect on me."

"What are you going to do, kill me?" she said it

with steel in her voice, but inside she was a puddle of fear. "It's not like you have an alibi in Dublin this time. If anything happens to me, my family will figure it out straight away."

She wasn't confident of this, but it felt good to give the impression of holding a bargaining chip.

"I'm not going to kill you," he muttered. "Now. I don't like you standing there. I know you lot are sneaky. Give me your phone and get over there behind the bar where I can keep an eye on you."

"I don't have it. It's upstairs—I was going to get it when you appeared like a ghoulish apparition."

His face fell before rearranging into a sly grin she really didn't like. "Really? You're going to slag me off when I'm standing in front of you with a knife? Give me your phone."

"I just told you. I don't have it."

"Where is it?"

She sighed. "On my bedside table I think. I'm not sure."

"Right," he said, shoving her forward roughly. "Show me your hands."

She held them up.

"And pull up that jumper. It's not hidden in the waistband of your shorts is it?"

She rolled her eyes. "You just surprised me. Why

would I be wandering around in the middle of the night with my phone in my waistband?"

"You weren't supposed to be wandering around at all!" he shrieked. "It wasn't part of the plan."

"Sorry. Maybe you should have told me the plan. We could have had a project meeting. Set the milestones for holding Fiona hostage while you rob her bar. I must warn you: I've feck all money in here. You're welcome to it, but it'll barely cover your train fare to Dublin."

"I'm not here to rob you, you mouthy little monster. Go on. Over there. To the bar."

He followed her behind the bar and glanced along the counter. "Right," he said, after appraising the situation. "Put your hand there."

He pointed to the brass rail that ran the length of the wooden counter. Fiona glanced around, seeing to her dismay that he hadn't just pulled from the lead of the phone: he'd cut the wire with scissors. *There goes my only lifeline to the outside world*, she thought.

He reached into the pocket of his fleece and pulled out something that shone in the light. Fiona's brain joined the dots and told her what it was, but she had to blink a few times to make sure she was really seeing them.

"Handcuffs? Where'd you get handcuffs?"

He flushed and turned away. "You think you're

very funny, don't you?" He lashed one side of the cuffs around her wrist and the other around the rail, pulling hard on it to make sure it was securely fastened to the bar.

Fiona's eyes widened. They weren't the kind of handcuffs you got in kids' cop play sets. Nor were they of the pink and fluffy variety. No, these looked very real. And judging from his reaction when she had asked him where he got them, Fiona had a brief moment of inspiration as to what Mrs Stanley had on the seemingly staid and upstanding Alan Power.

"The bedside table, you say."

She nodded. "It's only an old pile of rubbish," she muttered. "You won't even get ten euro for it on eBay."

"I'm not here to rob you, you idiot. How many times do I have to tell you?"

She turned away. His breath was sour and unpleasant, and he seemed intent on yelling into her face. It crossed her mind to ask him nicely if he could just go swish some mouthwash around his gob, but she didn't want to incense him more than she already had. She was beginning to take him seriously now she was stuck in the bar with him, with no help at hand.

"Yeah, it's on the bedside table."

"Good. I'll be back in a minute. Oh, they'll love

this. Getting a call from you and then finding out it's me. That'll teach them to mess with me!"

"Who?" she whispered, genuinely confused. "What are you talking about?"

"Your father!" he crowed. "Oh, they think they can blackmail me when I asked quite reasonably for proof that things were square between us. Well, I'm sure they won't mock me when I want proof in exchange for the safe return of their daughter."

"Ah." When he put it like that, there was a strange sort of sense to what he was saying. It was then that she realised she was in a lot more trouble than she thought.

"You know, it's actually a funny story. We were trying to get to the bottom of the murder. We found a Gmail account belonging to Mrs Stanley but we could only see one side of her conversations. I don't know what she had on you or any of the rest of them. It was all a fishing expedition."

His eyes narrowed. "Nice try. Are you sure you want to lie to me? There's no way I'm giving ye any money. I made that mistake once before. No, you need to just shut up and wait. And hope that your father and grandmother decide to do the right thing and hand me over all the copies of those photos."

Fiona shook her head. She was about to protest again when she realised there was little point. It was clear he'd fallen for their lies and wasn't going to believe they were bluffing.

Keep him talking, she thought suddenly. She didn't know what time it was, but if she could stall him for a few hours, then someone might pass and suspect…

The button.

The little doorbell that was wired through to the hardware shop.

Her relief was short-lived. There was no way Marty was going to be in work; not for at least another few hours. Could she stall Power and keep him talking for that long? She didn't have a lot of confidence.

But that was her only option. She took stock of her surroundings. There was a chopping board within reach—the knife she used for chopping limes must have been in the dishwasher at the other end of the bar. Otherwise there were straws and bar napkins. A box with numerous chalk pens and stickers she used to update the blackboard outside. In other words, nothing useful except for the bell.

"Stay there," he hissed. "Don't try anything funny."

She tried to smile as ingratiating as she could. "So how did you get to work in IT? Did you do computer science in college?"

He did a double take. "What?"

"You heard me. There's no money in bars. I've been thinking for a while about how I might go back to college and study something useful."

"I'm not a careers advisor," he sniffed, turning and stomping towards the door to the flat.

Left alone, Fiona pressed the buzzer to the hardware shop. She knew it was futile, but it felt better than doing nothing. In the silence of the night, she imagined she could even hear the faint buzzing sound through the wall.

She smirked. Mrs Davis on the other side wouldn't like that, she thought.

And then it struck her. She turned around, praying she had left it in its usual spot along with the controls for the heating system. Sometimes she carried it around with her when she was closing up.

She hissed a great sigh of relief. It was there alright. She pushed forward. She had about a metre of wiggle room along the section of the rail she was cuffed to. She jiggled the cuff right to the join and reached across.

Yes, she thought as her fingers closed around the remote control for the sound system.

Knowing she didn't have much time, she poked the power button. Then she turned the volume as loud as it would go and turned the remote over in her palm.

Music blared out of the speakers around the bar as she flipped the remote in her hand and awkwardly tried to remove the battery cover with one hand cuffed. It was so loud that the building seemed to be vibrating around her, but she told herself not to rest on her laurels just yet. After all, Power was surely on his way down.

Sure enough, he appeared at the door a moment later, his face the very picture of rage.

His lips moved, but there was no way she could hear his words over the thumping music. He marched across the floor and her shaking, sweating fingers fiddled with the cover until it finally came loose.

She wasted no time at all tipping the batteries into her palm and feeding them one-by-one down the sink. The last one dropped from her fingers just as Power reached her.

32

He pulled the remote from her hand and jabbed at the buttons before pausing to look at what he was pressing. Fiona tried not to look too smug: after all, she was cuffed to the bar and in the company of a mad man. And she wasn't even certain the plan would work.

After another few seconds, he stopped and pulled off the cover of the battery compartment. His lips moved again, but even standing close to him she couldn't hear him.

"What the hell did you do?" he screamed into her face. "That was stupid!"

Next, he hurried over to the wall where the largest speaker was mounted and frantically moved around it. Fiona knew he was looking for the plug.

This time, she couldn't help but allow herself a little smile. She had wanted to save money and place the speakers close to existing power outlets, but Marty had nagged her for days that it was a better idea to have the wires out of sight, especially in a bar where someone might spill a drink or attempt to pull the speaker out of the wall after a few too many. She had tried to convince him that her bar wasn't going to be the type to attract customers like that, but he'd been uncharacteristically insistent about it. She had agreed mainly to shut him up, and she had moaned for days about the cost of getting an electrician out to wire the speakers into the walls.

She wished she could hug Marty now. It was possible he'd bought her another few minutes—her plan might just work after all…

"Turn it off!" Power cried, red-faced and sweating.

"I can't!" she roared back, just as one song faded and the next came on. Her voice sounded startlingly loud in the silent pub.

"Well do if you know what's—" The music prevented her from hearing what he said next—not that she wanted to know.

Fiona's palms were beginning to sweat again. It had been silent when the music stopped. She had hoped it might have drawn attention, but there hadn't been a sound inside the pub or out of it.

It's not going to work, she thought. And if it's not…

She looked over at Power. He still had her phone in his hand. Knowing him—and she didn't really, but she'd seen enough of him to get the measure of the man—he would have wanted to make the call to her parents in her presence. She had deprived him of the opportunity—for now, at least.

But he'd figure it out. He had just completed a circuit of the bar, searching in vain to find a switch for the speakers. He marched over to her, angrier than she'd ever seen him.

"Where's the fuse board?"

Fiona shook her head. "The what?"

She knew well what he was talking about, but forced herself to play the fool.

"It's your bar. You must know where it is."

She shrugged. "I don't. Sorry."

The truth was it wasn't far from them at all. It was in the bar kitchen, right behind where they both stood.

The music must have been going for several minutes, she calculated. And still nothing had happened. Had she made a mistake? She hoped not —this was her last hope.

"I'm running out of patience with you!" Alan

Powers shouted, stepping from foot-to-foot, clearly in a panic.

"Well I'm not exactly brimming with patience at the moment either, to tell you the truth," she muttered, her voice totally drowned out by the music.

The next moment, his eyes lit up as if he'd been struck by inspiration. Fiona didn't like that look at all.

He hurried towards her, but instead of shouting, he reached under the bar for a glass.

"Move," he said, exaggerating the movements of his lips so she'd understand.

Fiona looked from his face to the glass and back, as it slowly dawned on her that he'd figured out a way to turn off the music. She flattened herself against the sink.

"Sorry, what? I can't hear you."

She was well aware of the knife in his hand, but she couldn't allow him to do it. True, he'd said he wouldn't harm her, but she doubted he'd be so calm when her father told him he couldn't hand over the photos because he didn't have them. There was simply no way he was going to believe that, and it wasn't as if he felt any goodwill towards the McCabes after they had kept him prisoner in his home earlier that evening.

"Move," he said, shoving her.

Fiona steeled herself to try and resist, but he was strong despite his paunchy, office-drone look and he soon shoved her out of the way.

She watched in horror as he filled the glass before hurrying across the floor. Her stomach lurched as he flung it at the speaker before scurrying away. The music seemed to slow down and become distorted. The speaker fizzled and cracked before there was a loud popping sound and the bar fell silent.

"There," he said, after he'd taken his hands away from his ears. "You thought you were clever, but I'm smarter than you. We can tell that to your father when we ring him, can't we?"

Fiona bristled with pure dislike as he walked towards her. The ruined speaker system continued to make popping sounds, but that was the least of her worries then. She wished she'd taken the few minutes to sit down and put a lock code on her phone. As it was, he was able to unlock the screen and access her contacts within a few seconds.

At least the lights hadn't been knocked out, she thought. As maddening as Alan Power was, she'd far rather be able to keep an eye on him than be left in the dark wondering what he was up to.

"Here we go. 'Dad', I presume."

"You're very smart, alright," she snapped.

His face scrunched up, but he returned his attention to her phone without saying anything. Her mind raced with possible ways to distract him, but she could think of nothing.

"These handcuffs seem well worn anyway," she said, trying to inject her words with a bravado she didn't feel.

He glanced up at her, eyes narrowing to slits. "Don't think you can mock me and get away with it."

She closed her eyes. This was either a very brave approach or a very stupid one, and she didn't have the benefit of hindsight to tell her which it was.

"Ah sure why wouldn't I? It's all around town, you know. Straight-laced IT professional with the secret dark side. You should have thought about that before you handed over your not-hard-earned euros to Mrs Stanley."

"What?" he spluttered. "You're lying. No-one knows."

She shrugged. "You keep telling yourself that."

He glared at her for a few seconds before returning his attention to her phone. "You're lying. Trying to bluff."

"If that's what you want to believe…"

This time, he didn't take his eyes away from her phone. She knew all was lost.

"Here we go. I can't tell you how much I've been looking forward to this call," he said, eyes gleaming.

Fiona's pulse raced as his index finger tapped the screen and she heard the dialling tone.

She didn't know whether she wanted her father to pick up or to not—it seemed like whatever happened, she was doomed.

The phone rang and rang and it seemed as if they were suspended in the silent, too-bright pub.

Then there was a loud groan. Fiona froze.

"Oh it's off now," she heard a very agitated voice say. "But it was so loud, Garda. It's not acceptable."

Fiona's heart swelled. She knew that voice—she'd already had a run-in with the woman behind it. But was it too late? Depending on who was out there with her, they might notice the silence and decide to leave it alone. She wasn't sure how Alan Power had managed to get in: now she hoped he'd had the decency to leave obvious signs of a break in.

Not only that, but the dialling tone stopped and the phone made a shrill beep sound before going silent. Francis McCabe had disabled his voicemail the week before, complaining that he didn't want to pay good money for the privilege of listening to telemarketers' nonsense.

Alan seemed to sense her optimism.

"We'll try him again in a few minutes," he

whispered. "And you better stay very quiet. No one knows I'm here and I'd like to keep it that way." He held up the knife. She didn't like the way it glinted in the light. She was still handcuffed to the rail—it wasn't like she could run for help, even though it sounded tantalisingly close at hand.

If only Mrs Davis would stick to her guns and demand that Fiona be taken to task for the noise. Fiona could never have imagined she'd be willing her neighbour to complain about her!

She closed her eyes and listened hard. It was silent out there now. She still had no idea which of the guards was out there with Mrs Davis. What if she'd decided to give up? The music was off. Maybe she had decided to let it go. Fiona's heart sank.

Time for a new plan, she thought.

"What time is it?" she asked Alan.

He opened his mouth to answer and then clamped it shut again. "I told you to be quiet," he muttered, barely moving his lips, like a very angry ventriloquist with a knife.

"Sorry," she whispered. "I just want to know the time."

His brow furrowed, but he did indeed glance at her phone. "You don't need to know," he muttered.

She sighed. It couldn't be more than an hour since she'd gone downstairs. That meant that Marty wouldn't be at work for another two hours. And realistically, it could be another three before he got to the shop.

Fiona's options were beginning to look very limited indeed.

"We'll try him again," Alan Power whispered.

"Can I at least make us a cup of tea?" It was a last desperate attempt and it was obvious from his face that he knew that.

"No. Just stand there and be quiet. Oh, look. It's ringing."

The sound of wood shattering drowned out the dial tone. Fiona leaned across the bar as much as she was able; staring in the direction of the door to see what was going on. It had been silent for several minutes: she had assumed Mrs Davis had left.

"Sorry, Miss McCabe," Garda Conway said, coming through the inner door. "But we've had reports of a disturbance of the peace. You can't play music at that volume in the middle of the night."

"No, you can't," Mrs Davis said, folding her arms and looking very reproachful indeed.

Fiona reached for the chopping board just in case Alan decided to try something stupid. She wiggled her other wrist so the handcuffs rattled.

"I couldn't think of any other way to call for help. He's handcuffed me here. And he's got a knife."

Garda Conway looked stoic. "I can see that alright. Hold on there, Fiona."

"It's not like I can go anywhere, is it?"

"No, indeed," Conway said. "I suppose not." He cleared his throat. "Now, son. We can do this the easy way or the hard way."

Fiona snuck a reluctant glance at Alan to see how he was coping with the pressure. He seemed stable, but she had no way of knowing for sure. He'd been half-mad *before* Garda Conway even arrived.

"Mrs Davis. Go outside and call Garda Fitzpatrick," Conway muttered.

Fiona's heart sank as she saw Alan Power take in this information. Then she caught sight of something else.

"Yeah," Fiona said loudly. "You tell Garda Fitzpatrick to get down here and arrest this man for breaking into my pub. Tell him to come right away before there's any more trouble."

Alan sneered. "I never broke in anywhere. I think you'll find that this big oaf here did the damage. Now." He took a step closer to her.

Fiona's heart leapt into her throat. "No. What are you doing? Can't you see? He's not armed."

"But Garda Conway," Mrs Davis protested. "I don't have Garda Fitzpatrick's number. I called 9-9-9 earlier. They warned me I shouldn't do that again unless it was an emergency."

"Go on, Mrs Davis," Garda Conway said, looking flustered. "Get outside. Tell them I said it was alright. I don't care how you do it: get Garda Fitzpatrick. Now!"

Fiona glanced at Power's hand. Her phone was still lit up. "You've a choice here Alan," she yelled, even though he was standing close to her. "If you come for me, they'll have backup here before you can uncuff me and get away. If you run now, you can get back to your car and be long gone before they come."

"Don't take me for a fool. You've cameras in this place. I can see them. How do I know they're not on a different circuit to the speakers? The lights never went out. You'll have me on camera."

"Maybe so," she said with a shrug. "Which means you're screwed either way. If you go, you might get on a ferry to England before they catch up with you."

"Fiona!" Garda Conway said sharply.

"She's right," Alan hissed, before turning and bursting away towards the flat and the back door that led out onto the street.

33

"WHAT ON EARTH WERE YOU THINKING?"

Fi shook her head, only half-focused on what he was saying. "I hope he got all that. I hope to God he didn't reactivate his voicemail in the time between Power first calling him and that call just now."

"What are you talking about?"

She shook her head. "Nothing. Come on. We have to go after him in case Dad didn't hear all that. Can you call him just to make sure?"

"I have more important things to do. Like catching that murderer before he gets away."

"He's not the murderer," she said, confused. "Why do you say that?"

Garda Conway said nothing, he just pointed at her hand.

"Oh this? Yeah, it's a long story. Can you get this cuff off me? And can I borrow your phone for a sec? Power ran off with mine."

"Where did you get these? They're real cuffs not those plastic things. Hold on. I should have a key here somewhere."

She waited impatiently as he searched his pockets. "They're not mine. They're his. And I don't know for sure but I have a good idea how he got them."

Mercifully, Garda Conway found a key and Fiona's hand was free at last. He handed her his phone and she dialled Colm's number from memory.

He answered within seconds.

Fiona didn't bother with formalities.

"It's Fi. Did Dad call you?"

"Mam did." His voice was high and distorted. She realised he was running.

"You're on the way to the place we were earlier?"

"Yeah."

"We'll meet you there."

She ended the call and nodded. "We'll be grand as long as he goes home. Dad's on the way there and so are my brothers."

Garda Conway winced. "He's armed with a knife."

"I wouldn't worry about them."

Mrs Davis made her way back into the pub with a pained expression on her face. "I had to ring directory enquiries. Those calls are very dear. I couldn't face ringing 9-9-9 again and having your one complain to me."

"Did you get through Fitzpatrick?"

"I did. He's on the way."

THEY DROVE in Garda Conway's car to Power's house in silence. Mrs Davis had been offered to stay behind and look after the bar. Fiona had awful visions of her pottering around the flat upstairs, gathering dirt on her to share at ICA meetings—or worse.

"Louise Graham is the murderer," she blurted.

She had almost forgotten that in the standoff with Power.

"What? So what was your man doing breaking in and threatening you?"

"It's a long story," she said, rolling her eyes. They were nearly there. "He was key to us finding out the truth."

Garda Conway nodded. "And have you?"

She smiled sadly. "It looks like it. I've no proof though."

"Proof exists?"

"It did at one stage. Mrs Stanley must have had pictures on her computer because Alan Power mentioned a picture of the sergeant with Bernard Boyle. Who would have thought that people actually handed over brown envelopes in real life? I thought that was a made up sort of thing. Surely they use bank transfers these days."

"Is that what he was at?" Garda Conway sounded resigned but not surprised. "Ah, sure you can't be making a bank transfer for a bribe. That leaves a trace, see."

They pulled up to Alan Power's house. Fiona was dismayed to see it was dark. The garage door was down so it wasn't clear whether Power had managed to get back and make a getaway or if he'd opted for a different plan, though she couldn't imagine him stealing someone else's car. Then again, she hadn't thought him capable of kidnapping either.

It was only when they got out of the car that they saw the shadowy figures on the lawn.

Francis McCabe sat across Power's chest; Colm sat across his legs. The man was completely immobilised; his knife a safe distance away on the grass.

The two McCabe men looked so calm and casual that they might as well have been sitting there having a lovely picnic.

"Garda Conway," Francis said.

"Francis. You got here fast."

He nodded. "I ignored the first call from Fiona but answered the second time. I was going to give out to her for calling so late, but then I heard what appeared to be a ruckus."

Fiona hugged her arms around herself. Her wrist was sore from the metal cuff that had been around it for hours. "It's lucky I saw the call had gotten through to you. He got distracted when Garda Conway came in."

"I sent Mrs Davis out to call for backup while I kept an eye on him. I didn't know what you were at, Fiona."

"I was trying to stop him going for me with that knife. I figured Dad was listening. To be honest, even if he wasn't I'd rather have Power away from me and not having a stand-off with you."

"Too right, love," Francis said, seeming to wiggle around on Power's chest. "We should have known the eejit might try something like that. Ah, if only we'd made you stay the night, love."

"It's alright, Dad. No one came to any harm."

"What about me?" Power wailed. "They're assaulting me as we speak. I hope you're going to do something about this, Garda."

Garda Conway walked over to where they sat.

Francis and Colm moved away as the officer rolled Power onto his front and cuffed him, making it look effortless. He got to his feet and dragged Power with him.

"I know you were only acting to get yourself out of danger, Fiona. But a little faith wouldn't go astray. I'd have got to him before he even considered hurting you, if it came to it."

Fiona smiled. "Sorry, Garda Conway. It was no slight to you. I just knew Dad would spring into action if I shouted enough information when he was on the line."

"Oh quit it you," Francis said, waving his hand and pretending to be disgusted though he was clearly delighted by his daughter's compliment.

"I'd better get this deviant back to the station," Garda Conway said, pushing Power in front of him. "I'll need a statement from you as well Fiona, but I'll give you an hour or two to get the pub fixed up." He shot her a significant look. "And we need to discuss other matters too."

She nodded and led the way along the path, ignoring the confused looks from her father and brother.

34

Mrs Davis was tucked away in the snug when they arrived back at the pub. She had a steaming cup of tea and a scone from the batch Fiona had made the day before. She was flicking through a magazine Fiona had left on her bedside table. There was no doubt in Fi's mind that Mrs Davis had had a good root through her belongings.

Mrs Davis glanced up and saw Fiona was staring at the magazine. "I got bored," she said defensively. "I've only an old brick of a phone. I don't be stuck on it like you young ones."

Fiona was resentful for a moment, but then a realisation hit her. If it hadn't been for Mrs Davis, she'd likely still be cuffed to the bar—or worse. That thawed her feelings somewhat.

"Thanks, Mrs Davis. Read away. You calling Garda Conway really saved my skin back there."

The older woman looked up and seemed to scrutinise her. A smile played at her lips—she appeared to be fighting it to the bitter end, but it won nonetheless.

"I cannot believe your strategy was to blare the music so I'd call the guards and complain. Am I really that much of an old biddy in your eyes?"

She was so close to the truth that Fi couldn't help but smile. "If you weren't an old biddy, that maniac might still have me as his prisoner. There's a lot to be said for being an old biddy."

Mrs Davis smiled. It was the first time Fiona had ever seen any warmth in her expression—at least when it came to her. "I suppose I'm set in my ways. I thought you were having some sort of rave."

"Sorry," Fiona shrugged. "He took my phone and cut the cord to the landline. It was the only way I knew of getting help." She looked around. "Where's Marty? Has he come in? I owe him too: if he hadn't nagged me about wiring the speakers into the wall, I'd have just got plug-in ones. Power would've had the music turned off within seconds."

Francis shook his head. "He went to the train station. We thought it was best to go our separate ways just in case Power decided not to go for his car."

"Good thinking."

"I see that expensive speaker system of yours is ruined," he said, after doing a tour of the place.

She shrugged. "And I'm going to have to get a plumber over to get the batteries out of the sink."

"What were you doing putting batteries in the sink?"

"I had to put them out of Power's reach."

"Maybe so," Francis muttered, moving behind the bar. "But you needn't be calling a plumber for that. I don't know what's wrong with you. All you need to do is get under the sink and pull out that section of the pipe. And you'd throw good money at a plumber?"

Mrs Davis nodded enthusiastically. Fiona yawned and rubbed her eyes. "I didn't realise, alright? It's not as if I've ever had to throw batteries down the sink to hide them from a madman."

Mrs Davis's ears pricked up. "What was he even doing here? Is he mad at you over some failed romance or something?"

"My goodness, Mrs Davis," said a cold voice from behind them. "How could you even suggest such a thing? My granddaughter is far too good for a fella like that. He's not only mad but he's got no respect for his elders. You'd never go near a young man like that, would you, love?"

Fiona spun around and hurried towards her granny, falling gratefully into a hug. "Granny. Mam told you?"

"Oh, love! She's been trying to get through to me for hours but I had the phone on silent. The notification sounds wake me during the night if I don't turn off the ringer. What's been going on? Come on, I'll make us a pot of tea and you can tell me everything."

"I've a pot on in the kitchen," Mrs Davis piped up. "And I'll take a hot drop if it's going."

35

THE PUB WAS STILL in a bit of a state when Fiona left an hour later, but her family had rallied round to sort the place out. Marty had already removed the blown out speakers and called an electrician in to check the wiring. Colm was in the process of fixing the lock on the front door and reinforcing the frame where it had splintered. And Mrs Davis was still in the snug, happily reading her magazine and proclaiming the bar not so bad after all for a young person's spot.

The Garda station was quiet when she arrived. She was relieved to see the sergeant hadn't arrived yet.

"I'll tell Conway you're here," Garda Fitzpatrick said. "He told me to let him know as soon as you arrived."

She nodded. "How are things going with Power?"

"As well as could be expected." He smiled. "He broke down after a few minutes and confessed to everything, though he did make some strange allegations about your family."

Fiona froze for a moment. The McCabes would be in serious trouble if they got charged with intimidation, no matter how good their intentions.

Garda Fitzpatrick smiled. "Of course, he's obviously a lunatic judging by his carry on earlier. I wouldn't worry about any unsubstantiated claims he might make. Go on in there. Garda Conway will be with you in a minute. Would you like a cup of tea?"

"Fiona," Garda Conway said, looking harassed.

It was a surprise to her, given Garda Fitzpatrick's sunny demeanour. She said as much.

He shook his head. "He doesn't know about my suspicions about the sarge."

"Oh," she whispered.

Sergeant Brennan's corruption hadn't exactly been front and centre in her mind that morning given everything else that had been going on.

"I know. Anyway. First things first."

She gave her statement about Power's break-in. It

didn't take long to pull together as she was mainly recounting information that she'd already told him earlier that morning. Besides, Power had crumbled under pressure and confessed to everything.

"Did he tell you what Mrs Stanley had on him in the end?" Fiona asked. "I only ever had my suspicions based on the handcuffs."

"Only that he was being blackmailed as a result of his membership of a *progressive* club. Progressive was his word of course. And you know, I could have pushed him but to be honest I don't want to know. I can only imagine what he got up to with those handcuffs."

Fiona winced. "Thanks for the mental image. Very nice of you."

He laughed and shrugged, but Fi could tell there was still tension beneath the humour. She leaned forward.

"It was Louise Graham, like I said earlier. I can't imagine there's any connection between her and the sergeant or Bernard Boyle, but I don't know."

Conway nodded. "And how did you come to know this?"

"I'm sure you know about our chat with Power."

"Yes, indeed," he said, holding up a finger and double-checking his dictaphone was off. "We'll keep that between ourselves."

"Well, he told us he'd arrived at Mrs Stanley's house on the day she was murdered. He intended to steal her computer then, see."

"Ah," Conway said, brow furrowing. "Now, that's something he didn't own up to."

Fiona frowned. She hadn't thought about finding admissible proof.

"Don't worry," Conway laughed. "We'll get it out of him in an official interview."

"Oh," she said, relieved. "Anyway, he was there. We asked why he didn't try to get in and help and he told us he ran away because there was someone in there with Mrs Stanley. A woman."

Conway gasped.

"I know. All of this could have been avoided if he'd only had the sense to call ye. I mean, it's come out about his secret... *whatever*... anyway, or at least it's going to. It's so cowardly. My mother went through endless hours of questioning because he was too selfish to call and provide a lead in a murder case.

"Anyway, he was very unhelpful when it came to telling us her age or anything about her. But he remembered she was moving her shoulder very strangely."

Conway nodded.

"It took a while. I only remembered just before Alan

Power appeared in the pub and cuffed me to the bar. I'm kicking myself now—it's so obvious. She was on Mrs Stanley's blackmail list. And the really annoying part is that I overheard her in the pub complaining about an injury to her... Now, I can't remember the name of the muscle she mentioned, but I should have remembered from the way she was moving her shoulder."

"I see," Garda Conway said. "Unfortunately that's all circumstantial. I hate to say it, but it seems we're reliant on Power identifying the woman he saw in the house. And I'm not even sure that would stand in court. Any lawyer worth their salt would tear him apart and accuse him of trying to lie in return for a softer sentence." He sighed. "And here was I thinking I was going to coast into retirement."

Fiona felt a tug of regret. "Don't retire, Garda Conway. You're the only decent one out of the lot of them."

"Ah now here. Don't be so syrupy sweet: it doesn't suit you."

She grinned. "You sound just like my father. Should I take that as an insult?"

He shook his head but didn't say anything. They both fell silent for a while as Fiona went over the details of the case in her head again for the umpteenth time.

"Wait," she whispered. "It all hinges on those Facebook accounts. Remember?"

"I remember. Nothing's changed."

"But it has! It's different now," she said, sitting forward with excitement. "You've got Power in there saying he was blackmailed. I'm sure if you lean on him he'll admit to seeing Louise Graham."

"I already told you that won't mean much in court. He's admitted to kidnapping you."

"But it's proof the blackmail is a thing. Come on, Garda Conway. Even if you're not going to investigate Mrs Stanley's fake account, you've got to admit there's likely some trace of communication on Louise's phone or computer."

He nodded. "And Power's testimony may not be enough to get a conviction, but it's likely to convince a judge to give us a search warrant for her house." He looked around before his expression darkened and he shook his head. "Thanks, Fiona. Of course we might have found her a long time ago if the sarge hadn't been so eager to keep this blackmail thing from surfacing."

"Have you any idea what he might have going on with Bernard Boyle?"

"I don't know for sure," Garda Conway said. "But I have a fair idea."

"What are you going to do? I suppose you can't do anything if it'll mess up your retirement plans."

He looked miserable, but he didn't say anything. Fiona thought she caught a glint of defiance in his eyes. She certainly hoped that was the case. He held her eyes for a long moment before he shook his head and started to get to his feet. "All I know is we've enough to be getting on with for now. I'd better hurry along if I want to claim my first murder solve and not lose it to you-know-who."

36

Time was on Garda Conway's side that morning. The sergeant was delayed. By the time he arrived at the station, Gardas Conway and Fitzpatrick were in jubilant form. They'd managed to execute a search of Louise Graham's home.

Though laptops and phones were their main target in the search, a false panel in the wardrobe in the box room revealed a cache of images that were very sordid indeed. Garda Conway's report noted that Ms Graham became quite hysterical when those were found and begged them not to put it on her record. She appeared not to suspect they were gunning for a more serious charge until later, when they found an incriminating series of messages with one Pete Smith. When her search history unearthed a search for fast-acting poisons, she finally broke and confessed everything.

She had no idea how Mrs Stanley had come across those pictures. She'd done them for a men's magazine in America on the strict understanding they wouldn't be put online or published in Europe. She'd almost forgotten about them... until the messages started coming. She'd paid off 'Pete Smith' but that hadn't stopped him from demanding more money from her, telling her that she'd never get a teaching job if those pictures were made public. At that point, she had panicked. She went to the drop-off point, but instead of putting the money in the bucket and leaving, she hid in the bushes.

She only really wanted to find out who Pete Smith was; to reason with them. But that had all changed when she spotted Mrs Stanley—the last person she would have accused of trying to blackmail her. Her granny had been friends with May Stanley, and Louise had taken it upon herself to call in on her family friend from time-to-time to do odd jobs for the woman. She'd never received a word of thanks for it, of course, and now this!

Before she knew it, Louise was spending her days plotting. She knew Mrs Stanley would never leave her alone but how could she get rid of her without anyone suspecting? A plan formed in her head when someone walked into the gym and asked if she'd heard about Mrs McCabe and Mrs Stanley fighting in the street. She hurried out and popped home to pick up some breakfast things. Then she went straight to Mrs Stanley.

May Stanley didn't suspect a thing: Louise had often brought her breakfast. Louise could barely contain her anger as she cooked up the food. Mrs Stanley sat there barking orders at her, ungrateful as usual and probably scheming up ways to get even more money out of her!

After it was done, she smashed the old woman's computer and set about finding her copies of the pictures. The messages had said there were copies everywhere. She'd had to tear the place apart! She knew Mrs Stanley didn't get many other visitors so she was able to take her time. Sure enough, it took her hours but she found one set shoved up the chimney, one set in a bag of out-of-date porridge and another taped under a drawer. When she was satisfied she'd found all the pictures, she snuck out. When she was safely home, she went online and used an online message service to send a tip-off to the guards in Ballycashel about Mrs Stanley, suggesting Mrs McCabe might have harmed her. She felt no remorse: to her it was clear Mrs Stanley would have bled her dry if she hadn't done something.

Alan Power was charged with kidnapping, though the Gardaí noted his cooperation in the murder case and asked for that to be taken into consideration during sentencing. His accusations against the McCabe family were never spoken about again, much to the disgust of Sergeant Brennan.

There was no mention of what Power had seen on Mrs Stanley's computer. Garda Conway had a quiet word with him, setting the scene for him to be recalled as a witness in any other cases, should that be necessary. Alan Power seemed to understand this as some kind of get out of jail free card if he testified against the sergeant. Garda Conway was repulsed by such a notion, but he wisely allowed the rogue former IT professional to go on believing whatever he wanted to believe. Oh, he didn't do it on account of the sergeant appearing in one of the photographs. If anything, Garda Conway wanted to bide his time and see what hard evidence came to light rather than let the sergeant know he was on to him.

So there were a number of aspects of the case that were never made public to the wider public in Ballycashel. Not that anyone noticed. The whole town was abuzz with the news that Mrs Stanley was a blackmailer and thief. Well, that is, everyone except for the other blackmail victims.

None of them knew that Mrs Stanley's computer

had been destroyed. Some of them even went so far as to flinch when Mrs Stanley's name was mentioned. Granny Coyle had a quiet word with Mrs Roche and she seemed satisfied with her friend's response, though she was reluctant to discuss the matter with anyone else. Fiona longed to put the others straight; to reassure them that the truth wasn't likely to come out—at least not in public. She held off, though: she felt it might be even more harrowing if they knew that she knew. She spent a lot of time dwelling on that over the coming days.

Not that she had much free time for thinking.

As well as agreeing on a new stereo system for the pub, Fiona had agreed to install a panic alarm system. Her mother was insisting on it. As money was tight, she had a series of appointments lined up with different security companies to go through the pub and quote prices for this system. Other than that, she was occupied with running the pub, devising a number of specials to try and make up for the revenue she'd lost by opening so sporadically.

"What about a quiz?" Mrs Davis piped up.

She had become something of a regular in the bar ever since the break-in. It was astonishing really: she had gone from looking at Fiona with absolute disgust to being warm and chatty. It was strange at first, but Fiona was starting to enjoy her company and look out for the door opening shortly after half four after Mrs Davis had had her afternoon tea.

"That sounds like a great idea," Fiona said, grinning and jotting it down on her notepad. "I'm sure I could get one of the lads to be quizmaster and Dad has a load of trivia books at home."

"Not too risky, so," Mrs Davis said.

"Exactly."

The bell above the door rang and a moment later, Gerry Reynolds appeared in the bar. Fiona nodded hello. He was something of a regular. He came in at least once a week and he had been asking for pints of Guinness every time, even though she didn't serve Guinness on draft.

She smiled as he asked for just that.

"Sorry," she said, without even having to think about it. "We don't have Guinness on draft."

"No Guinness?" He looked genuinely astonished even though he must have said the same thing fifty times. "Sure what kind of a bar are you?"

She rolled her eyes. "A bar. We don't have to serve Guinness, you know."

The bell went again and Granny Coyle came in and took a seat at the bar. Fiona shot her a grateful smile. It was a coincidence, of course, but it was still nice to have more people around for one of Gerry's visits.

He was the town hardman, and he made Fiona nervous even though he'd be affronted if he knew such a thing. He'd declared his intentions towards her, though thankfully he hadn't repeated them after she told him she was taken.

"Well it's a horrid shame," he went on. "We're in Ireland, after all. It's part of our culture."

Granny Coyle winked. "You know, young man, that's a good point. I think I'll have a pint of Guinness too."

Fiona shot her a look of disdain. So much for being relieved by her grandmother's presence. "Are you sure that's wise at your age?" she said sweetly. "It might be a bit too much."

"Listen to her! Is that any way to speak to a customer?"

Gerry shook his head, a stupid smile plastered all over his face. "Ah, she's grand. There's something very attractive about a feisty woman."

Fiona very nearly lost her grip on the glass she'd just picked up.

"How about a Moscow Mule. Can I have a Moscow Mule?" Granny Coyle continued.

"What's that now?" Gerry moved across the bar closer to Rose, looking genuinely interested in trying something new.

"Oh they're lovely. I tried them in Lourdes. Vodka and ginger with a bit of lime."

"Is that so? Lourdes you say." He cleared his throat. "How are things going with that German boyfriend of yours, Fiona?"

Fiona had to work to figure out what he meant for a moment. It had all been a ruse to get Gerry to stop hanging around the bar making puppy dog eyes at her. It had worked, too.

Before she could answer and say that Felix was as darling as ever, though, Granny Coyle piped up.

"German boyfriend? Not that I know of. Someone's been having you on, young man."

"No, Granny, it's—"

"I'd surely know about it if she was courting someone."

Fiona shot her a significant look. "You do. You've met him. At our intimate family dinners, remember?"

Granny Coyle shook her head. Her face was the picture of innocence. "No. That's never happened."

"Sure it has. You were there. You made your famous apple tart and he compared it to his mother's apfel strudel."

"Nope. You must have been dreaming."

Fiona sighed and turned to Gerry, dismayed to see the expectant look on his face. "She has a touch of the dementia you see. It's an awful thing."

Granny Coyle let out a horrified gasp.

"She doesn't know it, of course." Fiona patted her grandmother's hand. "There, now. It's okay. I'll mind you."

"So he's still on the scene."

She nodded. "Yeah. We're planning a weekend break to Berlin sometime soon."

"Oh is that so?" Mrs Davis said, popping her head up even though Fiona hadn't realised she was listening to the whole exchange. "In that case, you'll be needing someone to look after the bar."

"Yeah, I suppose," Fiona said slowly, looking from Mrs Davis to her grandmother. "Marty usually steps in."

"Well, I'd be happy to help. You just let me know. I've started opening the shop part-time now. Far less demand than there used to be."

"I will," Fiona muttered. "Thanks."

———

LATER ON, when the others had left, Granny Coyle finally lifted her attention away from her Sudoku and spoke. "Dementia, hah? That's lovely so it is."

Fiona shook her head. "It was an awful thing to say, but what could I do? You were denying my story about my German boyfriend left, right and centre. You know all about it, you were just being difficult."

"I suppose it was funny."

"You know why we told Gerry that. He was getting far too intense. It's better than me coming straight out and saying I don't want to go out with him. He scares me, you know that."

Rose rolled her eyes. "There's no need to get all het up about it. I wasn't thinking. I was just trying to amuse myself." She narrowed her eyes. "You're getting all pally with Mrs Davis."

Fiona shrugged. "She helped out after the break-in. She used to give me a hard time before, but she's being really nice now. I like her."

Granny Coyle waggled her finger. "You better now be thinking of making her some form of surrogate granny, you hear? You've only got one granny and I'm her."

Fiona snorted. "I've two. Or are you forgetting about Granny McCabe?"

"Ah that other one's a boring aul biddy."

"I thought you hated that word."

"I *do*. When it's used about me."

"I see. A bit of a double standard there so…?"

Granny Coyle smiled, but Fiona could tell there was something on her mind; something that weighed heavily. "Okay, you're my favourite granny. Just don't tell Granny Mc."

This had no impact on Rose's mood.

Fiona frowned. "What's wrong? You've a face on you like a wet weekend."

"Ah, I'm being silly."

"No you're not. Sure tell me if you want. I won't tell a soul."

"Ah, it's just... I've been bored. Retirement's not all it's cracked up to be. I don't want to be some aul wan sitting around staring up at a TV screen."

"But you're nearly eighty!"

"I'm in my mid-seventies, love. And I'm fed up with all this talk of ICA meetings and knitting patterns."

"Well," Fiona said, leaning on the bar and feeling overwhelmingly underqualified to offer any advice. She was, after all, failing in the career department herself. "What would you like to do? Do you have something in mind? Nobody's forcing you to knit, you know."

"They're not, indeed. And if you've ever seen the things I've knitted you'd understand."

Fiona stayed quiet, remembering the scarf Granny Coyle had knitted for her. There had been something strangely terrifying about the riot of reds, pinks and purples.

KATHY CRANSTON

"Sure didn't you have a great time in Lourdes? The lads told me you managed to get yourself into mischief. I swear Colm aged five years from worrying about you."

"Yeah, it was good craic I suppose. But…" she sighed. "There's only so much fun you can have with a crowd of old fuddy duddies."

"So what, they're too old for you? You don't have to hang around with older people—there's no law that says you have to."

"It's not that." Granny Coyle's eyes grew thoughtful—wistful, even. "I had a great time these last few weeks. It was a real challenge trying to make sense of what was going on and running around the place with you trying to find answers."

Fiona smiled. She could say the same thing herself now that everything was getting back to normal. It had felt good to put an end to the case that had been hanging over her mother's head.

"It was good, yeah. But I suppose it's the novelty of it more than anything. It's not your everyday occurrence here in Ballycashel."

Granny Coyle blushed. "What if it was?"

Fiona shivered and then burst into an involuntary fit of nervous laughter. "What, you're proposing to make murder a regular thing in Ballycashel? Are you out of your mind?"

314

"Of course I'm not!" Rose cried, but there was a strange grin on her face, replacing the sombre look she'd had not a few minutes beforehand. "No, I'm thinking the investigating side of things suited me. What do you think?"

"You want to become a guard?"

"Good God almighty I want no such thing! I'd be an ancient yoke by the time I finished the training. And can you imagine me working for a little pup like Brennan? No, I'm talking about..." she shook her head and laughed. "About becoming a private detective. What do you say?"

Fiona stared at her in astonishment. For once, she was lost for words.

"Look at that corruption thing, as one example. Garda Conway has no real appetite to investigate it. I, on the other hand, can't think of anything I'd like more than to get to the bottom of whatever's going on with Sergeant Brennan and Bernard Boyle. What do you think?"

Fiona shrugged. "I think you should go for it if it's what you want to do."

"No, I mean what do you think about joining me?"

"Joining you?"

Granny Coyle glared at her. "Obviously I can't just go off half-cocked and set up by myself. I'll need you to be my partner."

If Fiona had been speechless before, she was utterly stupefied now. "Your partner? In what, a detective agency? I don't have the first clue about that sort of thing."

"Ah, lookit. There's no need to be modest. You're talking to me. I know you well enough to know that—"

"I'm not being modest!" Fiona cried, laughing more at the absurdity of the conversation than from any sense of amusement. "I literally know nothing about that world. And I've got a pub to run."

Granny Coyle planted her elbows on the bar and pushed her long-forgotten puzzle book to one side. She looked earnestly at Fiona, and Fi had to admit that her grandmother looked livelier and more enthusiastic than she'd seen her look for a long time. And that was quite something: Granny Coyle had been on top form when they were investigating Mrs Stanley's murder.

"We've already established that it's a fool's game for you to open during the day. You can still run the pub in the evenings. I'll help you out, or we can hire someone. I'll have you know that I was the mastermind behind this place when your parents first married. Sure they didn't know the first thing about running a pub!"

"Neither did you," Fiona said mildly. "You worked in the civil service before you got married."

"Lookit, I'd been frequenting pubs since before—"

"The emergency?" Fiona offered, eyebrows raised.

"Less of your cheek! Anyway, I know a thing or two about getting the most out of this place. Think about it—we could set up a little office in the back room. It's perfect with the separate entrance back there. Although there is something old school and clichéd about someone coming and meeting their PI in the back of a dark pub."

Fiona shook her head in disbelief. "You have it all planned out! How do you even propose to start? Don't you need a licence?"

Granny Coyle shrugged. "That's detail we can sort out when we're getting ourselves up and running."

"It's kind of a key point…"

"There!" Granny Coyle said triumphantly. "You see? I'm a big picture kind of woman. You obviously have an eye for detail. We'll go far, I tell you."

Fiona shook her head. "I haven't even agreed to this yet! You've sort of sprung it on me."

The truth was, she was still reeling from the surprise of it, but a small part of her relished the idea of doing something so outlandish—well, that was if it was even possible. Could she juggle the pub with a business that was so different from anything she'd ever done before in her life?

"Well," Granny Coyle said, taking a sip of her Moscow Mule. "Don't leave me hanging for too long. I might just have to go find myself another business partner. Your sister for example."

Fiona baulked. "You'd never go into business with Kate. The two of you don't get along; never have."

Granny Coyle's eyes twinkled. "Who's to say?"

"You're just trying to play us off against each other," Fi said, making a mental note to speak to her sister and see if Granny Coyle had also mentioned the plan to her. "We're not little girls anymore. You can't play us like that."

"No," Granny Coyle said. "No, I suppose not."

"And I know for a fact that she's not into that whole business. You've heard her yourself loads of times. She wasn't interested in helping us investigate."

"Aha," Granny Coyle said. "See that's where you're wrong. It wasn't that she wasn't interested in solving crimes, it was that she didn't see the point in doing so much work without getting paid for it."

"I see… so you have spoken to her about this?"

For a moment, Granny Coyle looked like she was going to answer, but then she just smiled, finished her drink and grabbed her Sudoku book. She stood up off the stool.

"I'll give you a few days to think about it, love. But don't wait too long—I don't want you to miss out on the opportunity of a lifetime!"

And with that, she hightailed it out of the pub, leaving Fiona staring after her in a state of wild confusion.